As you probably guessed from the picture, Atticus closely resembles me! I mean me, Henry the cat, not me, Jennifer Gray, the author. I'm thrilled to have so many fans and wanted to let you know that my, I mean, Atticus's new adventure is even funnier and more exciting than the last one. Thanks Jennifer for turning me into an action-cat hero! And thanks, you guys, for reading.

Henry (and Jennifer)

Praise for Atticus

'Atticus is the coolest cat in the world. This is the coolest book in the world.'
Lexi, age 7

'Atticus Claw is fantastic because it has interesting creatures and characters. I especially like Atticus.'
Charlotte, age 8

'I think that this book is the best book I've ever read because it's so funny!'
Yasmin, age 10

'Fun and exciting, Atticus Grammaticus Cattypuss Claw is the most cutest. Once I opened it I just couldn't put it down.'
Saamia, age 9

'It's mysterious – it makes you want to read on.'
Evie, age 7

'I would recommend it to a friend.'
Mollie, age 10

'Once you start to read it you can't stop!'
Molly, age 8

ATTICUS CLAW
Goes Ashore

Jennifer Gray is a barrister, so she knows how to spot a cat burglar when she sees one, especially when he's a large tabby with a chewed ear and a handkerchief round his neck that says Atticus Claw. Jennifer's other books include *Guinea Pigs Online*, a comedy series co-written with Amanda Swift and published by Quercus. Jennifer lives in London and Scotland with her husband and four children, and, of course, Henry, a friendly but enigmatic cat.

By the same author

ATTICUS CLAW
Breaks the Law

ATTICUS CLAW
Settles a Score

ATTICUS CLAW
Lends a Paw

JENNIFER GRAY

ATTICUS CLAW

Goes Ashore

ff

FABER & FABER

First published in 2014
by Faber and Faber Limited
Bloomsbury House, 74–77 Great Russell Street,
London WC1B 3DA

Printed in England by CPI Group (UK) Ltd, Croydon, CR0 4YY

A CIP record for this book
is available from the British Library

ISBN 978–0–571–30531–5

2 4 6 8 10 9 7 5 3

To Archie
With special thanks to Susan, Hamish and Henry

Atticus Grammaticus Cattypuss Claw, once the world's greatest cat burglar and now a police cat sergeant, was on beach-tidying duty at Littleton-on-Sea with the kittens from the local cats' home. The cats' home was where Atticus had done his first bit of community police-catting. His job was to teach the kittens how to stay out of trouble and do good things instead. It had taken them a while to get the hang of it but Atticus was pleased to see that all his hard work had paid off. Most of the kittens were meowing enthusiastically. They were keen to get started.

It was early morning. Atticus squinted at the sky. It was going to be a beautiful day. The sun was beginning to shine through the mist and the calm sea was turning from a flat grey to a sparkling blue. The beach would be busy later and Atticus wanted to help make sure everyone had a great day out by keeping the sand rubbish-free.

Atticus enjoyed his work as a community police cat. It beat cat burgling any day, even if it meant litter picking. Cat burgling was lonely work. When Atticus did it, he'd never had a proper home. He had to go from one job to another and adopt a new temporary human each time and pretend to himself that he didn't really mind when he did. True, he got paid in sardines and travelled to lots of exotic places like Monte Carlo, but it didn't really make up for the fact he didn't have a family.

Luckily for Atticus everything changed when he came to Littleton-on-Sea to do some burgling for Jimmy Magpie and his gang of thieving birds. That was when Atticus met the Cheddars and decided to stop being a cat burglar and start being a police cat instead. Now he lived with Callie and Michael and their parents, Inspector Cheddar and Mrs Cheddar. And he didn't just have a family. He had

loads of friends as well. His best friends were Mr and Mrs Tucker who lived at Toffly Hall and Mimi, the pretty Burmese. Mimi was the most sensible cat Atticus had ever met as well as the prettiest. He was looking forward to meeting her by the beach huts later and going for a stroll.

'You start that end,' he told one group of kittens. 'The rest of you come with me.' Atticus straightened the red handkerchief he wore round his neck, gave his police-cat badge a quick rub and set off briskly towards the pier, the kittens trotting behind him.

It seemed strange going back to the pier. The pier was the first place Atticus visited when he arrived in Littleton-on-Sea almost exactly a year ago. It was where the magpies had their nest. It was where they hid the stolen jewellery before Atticus told them to take it back.

The tide was out just like it had been on that first day. Atticus picked his way between the clumps of seaweed. It was dark under the pier, and gloomy. He gazed up at the iron rafters. The sunshine came in stripes through the wooden planks. Yes, there it was, the magpies' old nest – a

messy heap of twisted twigs, just as he remembered. He wondered where Jimmy, Thug and Slasher were now.

Atticus's whiskers twitched. Last seen, the three magpies and their mates had been trying to escape from a plague of locusts in an Egyptian pyramid along with Atticus's old enemy Ginger Biscuit – a horrible tomcat who had once chewed Atticus's ear when he was a kitten. Unfortunately Biscuit and the magpies had got away. So had Biscuit's evil owner, Zenia Klob, Russian mistress of disguise. She was believed to be in hiding, possibly dressed as a melon seller. No one knew if the villains were still in Egypt. There had been no sign of them for several months. Interpol were still on the look-out.

'Recycling in the blue bag; rubbish in the black one,' Atticus told the kittens briskly.

One of them yawned. 'This is boring!' he said. 'I want to have an adventure, like you. I want to catch a criminal.'

The kitten's name was Thomas. He was a tabby,

4

like Atticus. He'd once got into trouble with Inspector Cheddar for stuffing a ball of wool up the exhaust pipe of Inspector Cheddar's panda car, and ripping the seats. He reminded Atticus a lot of himself when he was a kitten.

Atticus looked stern. 'Thomas,' he said. 'I've told you – adventures are dangerous. Criminals are bad news. Beach tidying is much more fun.' Even as he said it, Atticus realised he didn't sound very convincing. Beach tidying might be better than being a cat burglar but it wasn't much fun compared to having an adventure. Thomas was right.

Thomas wandered off to one of the iron pillars to sulk. The other kittens collected a few ice-cream wrappers and an old bucket and threw them into the rubbish.

Atticus glanced round. 'Thomas, can you grab that?' he called. A squashed blue and white parcel rested against the base of the pillar. 'Look. Just there.'

Thomas slouched towards it. 'Ergh!' He prodded the parcel with one claw. 'I'm not picking that up.'

Atticus marched over to take a look. He grimaced: the squidgy parcel was an old nappy.

'You do it,' Thomas said cheekily. 'You're the police cat.'

Atticus glared at him. Cats are very clean animals and Atticus was no exception. The thought of touching a nappy with one of his lovely white paws or, even worse, picking it up with his shiny white teeth made Atticus's stomach squirm. But he had to set an example. That was what community police-catting was all about. Inspector Cheddar had made that very clear. And Inspector Cheddar sometimes got cross with Atticus if he didn't do as he was told.

'Okay,' Atticus snapped. 'Susan and Hamish, hold the black bag open.'

Two other kittens came forward and held the bag.

Atticus took up a position on the other side of the nappy, facing away from it. 'Ready?' he called.

'Yes!' the kittens replied.

'Aim!' Atticus planted his two front paws firmly and braced himself. He wriggled his back paws into the sand under the nappy, being careful not to touch it. 'Fire!' He kicked backwards with his powerful hind legs. The nappy flew up into the air

6

and landed in the black bin bag. He turned to Thomas. 'If you want to have adventures you need to be able to deal with a dirty nappy,' he observed.

Thomas looked surly.

'Right, I think we're all done here.'

'Wait!' it was Thomas again. 'There's something else.' He pointed to the spot where Atticus's hind legs had flicked the sand.

Something glinted in one of the stripes of sunlight. For a moment Atticus thought it might be one of the jewels he had stolen for the magpies, which had fallen out of the nest. But then he reminded himself that all the jewels – every single one of them – had been returned to their owners when the magpies were arrested. It must just be another bit of rubbish.

'I'll get it,' Thomas said eagerly. He didn't look surly any more.

'Okay.' Atticus was pleased. Thomas seemed to have learnt a lesson.

'Maybe it's treasure!' Thomas scampered towards it.

Or perhaps he hadn't. Atticus sighed. He didn't want to disappoint Thomas but sooner or later the

kitten would have to learn that adventures didn't come along just because you wanted them to.

Thomas dug around the shiny object and pulled it out with his paws. 'It's just an old bottle,' he said in disgust, throwing it down again.

This time Atticus didn't tell Thomas off. He felt sorry for him. 'Green bag, please.' Atticus picked up the bottle carefully with his paws ready to put it into the recycling. It was then he noticed there was something inside it.

Atticus squinted at the bottle. It was dark green with a rubber stopper. On the side was a remnant of a label, which read:

Thump . . . Trad . . .
Beard . . .
D . . .

Thumpers' Traditional Beard Dye! Atticus stared at it in surprise. Mr Tucker used Thumpers' Traditional Beard Dye to dye his beard-jumper! *Maybe the bottle had once belonged to him?*

Mr Tucker was a fisherman. He was very proud of his beard-jumper. His beard had got mixed up with his jumper (or the other way around) when he was a baby and he'd been growing it ever since. That was until it got mangled in a nasty incident with Ginger Biscuit and the magpies. Fortunately, after a lot of failed experiments, Mr Tucker had invented a special beard-jumper potion, which made it grow back bushier and woollier than ever. In fact, it was so bushy and woolly that Mr Tucker had been nominated to host this year's World Beard-Jumper Competition. It was due to take place at Toffly Hall the next day. Mrs Cheddar was in charge of the organisation.

'Can I uncork it?' Thomas asked. He held out a paw. 'Please?'

'Okay but be careful you don't get anything on your fur,' Atticus said with feeling. Mr Tucker had once dyed Atticus white with Thumpers' Traditional to fool the magpies. The memory of it was still painful. He watched as Thomas pulled the rubber stopper from the bottle with his teeth.

'There's a bit of paper inside.' Thomas held the bottle out to Atticus. 'Maybe it's a message?'

Atticus doubted it. But, like Thomas, the bottle and its mysterious contents had made him curious. This *was* how adventures started. Perhaps wishing for them did make them happen after all! Atticus pinged out a claw, reached into the bottle, hooked the scrap of paper and pulled it out carefully.

The paper was thick and yellow, like something from an old storybook. The edges were rough, as if it had been torn from a bigger piece. Atticus unrolled it and smoothed it on a rock so that everyone could see.

The kittens crowded round.

'I told you!' Thomas cried.

Atticus squinted at the paper. It *was* a message! Thomas was right. Someone had scrawled across it with a blunt pencil in bold capitals.

'What does it say?' The kittens mewed. Not all of them could read yet.

Atticus read it out loud.

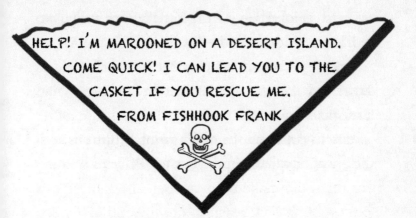

HELP! I'M MAROONED ON A DESERT ISLAND.
COME QUICK! I CAN LEAD YOU TO THE
CASKET IF YOU RESCUE ME.
FROM FISHHOOK FRANK

'I knew it!' Thomas shouted.

Atticus felt his heart beating fast. It definitely felt like the start of an adventure, but the message posed more questions than it answered. *Where was the island? What was in the casket? Who was Fishhook Frank? And what was that strange picture of the skull and two bones in the corner?* Atticus felt he'd seen it before, although he couldn't remember where. It certainly *seemed* familiar. He examined it carefully. The skull's empty eyes looked straight back at him. He shivered and turned the message over. On the back was a map of an island in the middle of a sea with squiggly lines and numbers scribbled all over it.

'Well?' said Thomas. 'What shall we do now?'

Atticus looked up. All the kittens were staring at him expectantly.

'Let's go and show it to Mr Tucker,' Atticus suggested. 'He's a sailor. He's bound to know what it means.'

Atticus collected the other group of kittens and they headed off to get the bus to Toffly Hall.

At Toffly Hall Mrs Cheddar was hanging up the banner for the World Beard-Jumper Competition with Mrs Tucker when Atticus stepped off the bus with the kittens. Each woman was perched on a tall stepladder at one of the gateposts.

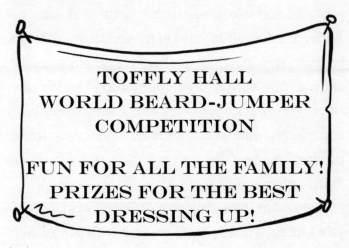

TOFFLY HALL
WORLD BEARD-JUMPER
COMPETITION

FUN FOR ALL THE FAMILY!
PRIZES FOR THE BEST
DRESSING UP!

'Left a bit!' Mrs Cheddar said. She looked down. 'Oh, hello, Atticus! You're just in time.'

Just in time for what? Atticus hoped Mrs Cheddar wouldn't ask him to help hang the banner. He couldn't stand heights. Besides, the preparations for the beard-jumper competition would have to wait. Atticus had a feeling the message in the bottle was much more important. Mimi called it instinct: that funny feeling you got when you just *knew* something without being told. He started meowing loudly.

'Not now, Atticus,' Mrs Tucker said crossly. 'Can't you see I don't have any sardines on me at the moment?'

Atticus's chewed ear drooped. The problem with humans was that they expected cats to understand English but *they* never made any effort to understand Cat. They always assumed when he started meowing that he wanted food when very often he was trying to tell them something completely different. (Actually, at that particular moment he wouldn't have said no to food, but that wasn't the point.)

'Go and find the children, Atticus,' Mrs Cheddar said kindly. 'They're up at the hall with Mr Tucker, sorting out the prizes for the fancy dress. I'm sure they'll have a snack for you. Then they'll find you something to do.'

The children! That was a good idea. Atticus hurried up the drive. The bottle, which was tied in the flap of his red handkerchief, clunked against his neck. The kittens chased after him, playing around his legs.

'Atticus!' Callie greeted him at the front door.

The kittens tumbled into the house and made straight for the sitting room to watch TV. All except Thomas, who remained with Atticus.

'We were hoping you'd be back soon!' Callie said, bending down to pick Atticus up. Atticus backed away. It wasn't that he didn't want a cuddle: it was more that he was worried the bottle might smash if it dropped on the floor. And he didn't want to look babyish in front of Thomas when he was supposed to be police-catting.

'Oh, I get it!' Callie seemed to understand. She rubbed his ears instead. 'Wait, what's this?' Her fingers felt the handkerchief.

Atticus lifted his chin so that she could remove the bottle.

'Michael!' she called. 'Come and look what Atticus has brought!'

Atticus purred. At least Callie realised it was important. Children were clever, like cats.

'A message in a bottle!' Michael took the bottle from his sister carefully and examined it. 'Where did you find it, Atticus? On the beach?'

Atticus purred louder. Then he remembered that technically it was Thomas who found the bottle, not him. He nudged the kitten forward.

'Thomas found it?' Callie picked Thomas up. 'Well done, Thomas!'

Atticus's good ear drooped. He wasn't used to sharing Callie and Michael with other cats. He didn't like it very much.

'Let's go and show Mr Tucker,' Michael suggested.

The children shot off across the hall with Thomas. Atticus scrambled after them, his paws slipping on the polished floor.

Mr Tucker was in the kitchen. He was standing on a stool leaning into a cupboard.

'What are you looking for?' Callie asked, putting Thomas down.

Mr Tucker jumped in surprise. The stool wobbled dangerously.

Atticus backed away. Mr Tucker had a wooden leg. Many years ago a giant lobster had clipped his real leg off when he was out on his boat. He could topple at any moment.

Mr Tucker regained his balance. 'I's not looking for anything,' he hissed. 'I's hidin' me beard-jumper potion. In case any of those rascals comin' to the competition try and get their hands on it.' He closed the cupboard and clambered off the stool.

'The other fishermen wouldn't steal it,' Michael said. 'Would they?'

'I's not talkin' about the other fishermen,' Mr Tucker said darkly. 'I's talkin' about the pirates.'

'Pirates!' Callie gasped.

'Aye, pirates,' Mr Tucker said tetchily. 'Who else did youze think would be comin' to a beard-jumper competition? Apart from fishermen.'

Atticus was listening intently to the conversation. *Pirates?!* He wondered if Mrs Tucker knew.

'Does Mrs Tucker know?' Michael enquired.

Mr Tucker went bright red. He didn't say anything.

'She doesn't, does she?' Callie persisted.

'She doesn't need to,' Mr Tucker blustered. 'That's why we's havin' the prizes for the fancy dress, see? So when the pirates come Mrs Tucker doesn't know they's *real* pirates: she just thinks they's in fancy dress!'

'But . . .' the children said together.

'And don't tell her!' Mr Tucker said crossly. 'Or she'll cancel the whole thing.'

Atticus felt his fur prickle. He knew about pirates. Michael and Callie sometimes read pirate stories to him at bedtime and he'd watched movies about them on TV when everyone was out. Atticus didn't like the look of them. Pirates had swords and eye patches and bad teeth. They made people scrub decks and walk the plank. He didn't feel very comfortable at the thought of them wandering round Toffly Hall pretending to be in fancy dress.

The children didn't seem too sure about it either.

'Maybe we should tell Dad?' Callie whispered to her brother. 'In case there's any trouble.'

Inspector Cheddar was in charge of security at the World Beard-Jumper Competition. Atticus knew for a fact he wasn't expecting 'any trouble' because Atticus was the only other police officer coming. Everyone else was going to Scotland Yard for a day out with Inspector Cheddar's boss, the Chief Inspector of Bigsworth.

Mr Tucker overheard her. 'Don't, Callie!' he pleaded. 'Your dad'll 'ave 'em all arrested before you can say "shiver me timbers".' He sat down heavily on the stool. To Atticus's horror a fat tear trickled down his cheek and dropped on to his beard-jumper. 'Youze don't knows what this means to me,' Mr Tucker sobbed. 'I's always wanted to host the World Beard-Jumper Competition ever since I was a baby. There was never room at the cottage. This is me big chance.'

(Mr and Mrs Tucker used to live in a cottage by the sea until Atticus came along. Thanks to him they discovered they had a priceless ruby necklace in the attic and bought Toffly Hall instead.)

'Please!' Mr Tucker wailed.

Atticus jumped into Mr Tucker's lap. Poor Mr Tucker! He seemed really upset. Besides, there were a few tasty morsels of fish lurking in his beard-jumper, which needed to be removed before the competition to make him look smart. Atticus started picking at it with his claws. Mr Tucker stroked Atticus absently. Atticus's presence seemed to soothe him. He stopped sobbing.

'I suppose so,' Callie said reluctantly.

'As long as you *promise* they won't do anything bad,' Michael added.

'Of course they's won't!' Mr Tucker beamed. 'They'll be as good as gold. The only one as would cause any trouble isn't on the guest list. I left him off on purpose.'

'Who's that?' Callie asked.

'Captain Black Beard-Jumper.' Mr Tucker shivered. 'The most fearsome pirate on the sea. He's got the biggest beard-jumper known to chins.' He winked at Atticus. 'With him out of the picture, I should win the competition!'

'I'm still not sure . . .' Callie hesitated. 'What do you think, Michael?'

'I don't know,' Michael said. 'Let's ask Atticus.

He's the police cat. What do you think, Atticus? Should we tell Dad about the pirates?'

Atticus thought for a moment. On the one paw Inspector Cheddar probably ought to know if Littleton-on-Sea was going to be besieged by pirates. On the other paw, if he did know, he'd tell Mrs Tucker, Mrs Tucker would cancel the beard-jumper competition and Mr Tucker would be sad. Atticus wriggled uncomfortably. *Help!* He didn't know what to do! It was much harder being a police cat than people realised.

'Well?' Michael said.

'Please, Atticus!' Mr Tucker begged. 'I promise everything will be fine.'

Atticus decided to side with Mr Tucker. It seemed as if he had it covered. Everything would be okay as long as Black Beard-Jumper didn't find out he hadn't been invited and turn up unexpectedly, like the bad fairy in Callie's Sleeping Beauty story. And that wasn't very likely to happen, was it? Atticus began to purr.

'Atticus says it's okay!' Mr Tucker cried.

'All right,' Michael said slowly. 'I guess that means we won't tell Dad.'

'I hope you're right about this, Atticus.' Callie frowned.

Atticus stopped purring. *So did he!*

'Thanks, Atticus, I knew youze wouldn't let me down!' Mr Tucker pulled two sardines out of his pocket. He gave one to Atticus and the other to Thomas, who had been waiting patiently by Mr Tucker's foot. 'Youze must be hungry after all that beach tidying!'

Atticus gulped the sardine down gratefully and cleaned his whiskers.

'Talking of beach tidying,' Michael remembered, 'Atticus found this.' He handed the bottle to Mr Tucker.

'Well, Thomas did,' Callie corrected. 'It's got a message in it.'

'A message in a bottle?! Well done, Thomas!' Mr Tucker pulled out a third sardine and gave it to the kitten. 'Youze got to be smaaarrrt to spot one of those.'

Atticus looked on in dismay. It wasn't fair! Now Mr Tucker was giving Thomas extra sardines!

22

Atticus was beginning to regret letting the children know that Thomas found the bottle. It wasn't really true anyway. If it hadn't been for Atticus, they wouldn't have gone to the pier in the first place! The bottle would still be buried under the nappy.

'Thumpers' Traditional Beard Dye?!' Mr Tucker twisted the bottle in his fingers. 'I'd say that means this message was sent by either a fisherman or a pirate. They's the only people who use Thumpers'.'

Apart from Zenia Klob, Atticus thought sulkily. She used it for her disguises.

Mr Tucker took a pair of tweezers from his pocket and pulled the message out.

The kittens watched intently. So did Atticus. He was annoyed to see that Thomas had jumped on to Mr Tucker's lap to get a better view. He was such a copycat!

Mr Tucker spread the paper out carefully on his good knee and read the message. His expression changed. Mr Tucker went red, then blue. He ended up a sort of funny combination of both, which Atticus thought might be called magenta. His whole body shook. He seemed to be having some sort of fit.

Thomas jumped down in panic.

The paper fell from Mr Tucker's knee and fluttered on to the floor, face up. Atticus took a second look at it. The picture jumped out at him. There was definitely something familiar about it.

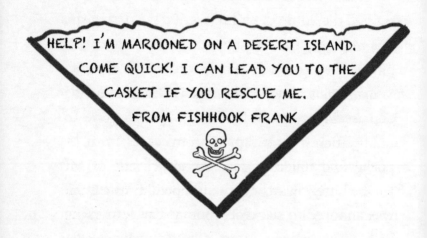

HELP! I'M MAROONED ON A DESERT ISLAND.
COME QUICK! I CAN LEAD YOU TO THE
CASKET IF YOU RESCUE ME.
FROM FISHHOOK FRANK

'Mr Tucker?' Michael cried. 'Are you all right?'

'What is it, Mr Tucker?' Callie shook his arm.

Mr Tucker's eyes were focused somewhere in the distance. 'The Caarrsket of Desires,' he whispered eventually. 'Fishhook Frank's found it at laaarrrst!'

'What's the Casket of Desires?' Michael shut the kitchen door behind Thomas, who had gone to join his friends in the sitting room.

The two children sat down either side of Mr Tucker at the table. Atticus jumped on to a chair beside Callie. He wanted to know what was going on.

The message lay in front of them on the table.

'I's not saying anything,' Mr Tucker said firmly. Callie had made him a mug of tea. Mr Tucker clasped it in his shaking hands.

'You have to tell us,' Callie said.

'Ooorrr what?' Mr Tucker frowned.

'Or we'll tell Dad about the pirates,' Michael said smartly.

'All right then,' Mr Tucker grumbled. 'I'll tell youze. But you'd better promise to keep it a secret.'

Mr Tucker seemed to have a lot of secrets today, Atticus observed. Callie lifted him on to her lap so that he could listen. Atticus purred gently. He felt loads better. He realised it had been silly of him to be jealous of Thomas.

'A long time ago,' Mr Tucker began, 'in a land far away, there lived an old woman . . .'

'It's not bedtime, Mr Tucker,' Michael interrupted.

'D'youze want to know about the caarrsket or not?' Mr Tucker glared at him.

'Sorry,' Michael said.

Atticus snuggled closer. He liked stories. This sounded like a good one.

'The old woman was very poor,' Mr Tucker continued. 'She lived in a tiny shack beside the sea. One day when she was out searching for sea slugs for supper, she found a mermaid washed up on the beach.' Mr Tucker put on a dainty voice. ' "Put me back in the sea," the mermaid begged the old woman, "and I will grant any wish you may have." '

Atticus listened intently. He wondered what he

would do if he came across a mermaid when he was on beach-tidying duty. He wasn't sure if he'd be strong enough to put her back on his own. Mermaids were big, like humans. Maybe the kittens would help.

'The old woman started to pull the mermaid towards the sea,' Mr Tucker went on. 'Then she stopped. "How do I's know youze won't just swim away if I's let you go?" she asks. "I promise that when I hear this rhyme," the mermaid says, "I will answer it at once:

Magic mermaid on the shore,
Please grant me what I'm wishing for."'

Magic mermaid on the shore, please grant me what I'm wishing for. It was quite catchy. Atticus thought he might try it next time he went to the beach, to see if a mermaid appeared. Except there wouldn't be much point in asking her for a wish because he already had everything he wanted, except more sardines. He turned his attention back to Mr Tucker.

' "Now put me back!" the mermaid sobbed. But

the old woman had thought of a way to trick the mermaid. "So," she says slyly, "youze promise that when  youze hear the rhyme you'll grant a wish?" "Yes!" the mermaid says . . .' Mr Tucker paused to light his pipe. He took a deep puff and exhaled loudly . . . ' "I promise! Now put me back! Or I'll die!" The mermaid couldn't breathe, you see,' he explained.

Atticus knew how the mermaid felt. Mr Tucker's pipe smoke wafted round the kitchen in a blue fog.

Michael opened the back door.

'What happened?' Callie coughed. 'Did the old woman put the mermaid back?'

'Yes,' Mr Tucker replied. 'She did. Then, when she saw the mermaid was strong enough to swim she summoned her with the rhyme.'

'Magic mermaid on the shore, please grant me what I'm wishing for,' Callie and Michael said together.

Mr Tucker nodded. 'Straight away the mermaid pops her head out of the water. "What is it you wish for?" she asks. And the old woman says, "I wish for a huge banquet." "Very well," says the mermaid and disappears into the sea. When the old lady returned to the shack she found the table was piled high with delicious food. Her wish had come true! She sat down and ate a whole cow.'

Mr Tucker placed his pipe in front of him and took a slurp of tea. Luckily some of it dribbled down his beard-jumper on to the tobacco. The pipe went out with a hiss.

Atticus nestled against Callie. He was mesmerised. He'd never heard such a good story before.

'The next day, the old lady went back to the beach and summoned the mermaid again,' Mr Tucker said. 'The mermaid pops her head out of the sea in surprise. "What do you want?" she asks. "I granted your wish yesterday." The crafty old woman grins. "You promised *when you hear the rhyme you'll grant a wish*," she winks as she quotes the mermaid's promise back at her. "Well, I just said the rhyme, didn't I? That means you've got to grant me *another* wish."'

Atticus's whiskers twitched. That old woman was a greedy pig.

'That's so mean!' Callie exclaimed.

'Aye,' Mr Tucker flicked his teeth in and out. 'As cunning as a crocodile, that old moo.' He sighed. 'The poor mermaid was horrified. She realised the old woman had tricked her. And now she was her slave. Every time the old woman said the rhyme, she would have to grant her a wish.'

Atticus could imagine Zenia Klob doing something sneaky like that. He wondered vaguely if she and the old woman were related.

'But why did the mermaid have to do what the old woman said?' Michael asked in a puzzled voice. 'Why didn't she just swim away?'

Mr Tucker sucked his pipe. 'The mermaid made a promise, see? And according to pirate lore a mermaid always keeps her promise.'

Atticus was puzzled. Pirate *what*?

Michael noticed his expression. 'Pirate lore means pirate legend, Atticus,' he told him. 'You know – stories that have been passed down from pirate to pirate.'

'Aye,' Mr Tucker confirmed. 'Over hundreds of years. That's what I's tellin' youze now.'

Atticus frowned. *How did Mr Tucker know so*

much about pirates? First they were turning up at Toffly Hall for the World Beard-Jumper Competition. Now he was recounting their legends! Atticus regarded him suspiciously.

'Where was I?' Mr Tucker grumbled. 'Oh yes . . . Every day after that the crafty old woman went to the beach, summoned the mermaid and made a wish. She wished for a palace to live in; she wished for fine clothes to wear; she wished for more jewels and gold than anyone else in the kingdom. Eventually the mermaid got together with all the other magical sea creatures in the world and begged them to help her. "You must hide yourself away," they told her, "in a place where the old woman can't find you." "There is no such place," the mermaid wept. "That old bat has enough money to buy a hundred ships to search the sea for me from one end to another." "Then we will guard you," the sea creatures said. "We will destroy her ships so she can never get close enough to summon you." To be on the safe side the sea creatures told the mermaid to put herself to sleep for a thousand years. "That way," they said, "the old woman will be dead and the rhyme will be forgotten. Neither she nor anyone else will be able to summon you ever again." '

A thousand years! Atticus liked sleeping but that was a long time for a nap, even by cat standards.

Mr Tucker was nearing the end of his story. ' "Is there no other way I can be free?" the mermaid said sadly. "No," the sea creatures said. "There is no other way." So the mermaid decided to take their advice. She locked herself in a glass caarrsket . . .'

'The Casket of Desires!' Callie squealed.

Mr Tucker nodded . . . 'and put herself to sleep. The sea creatures took the caarrsket and hid it in a secret lagoon. Then they patrolled the sea, waiting for the old woman to come.'

'What happened next?' Michael asked.

Mr Tucker drained his tea. 'When she found the mermaid had gone the old woman was furious. She bought a fine ship and sailed to the four corners of the earth searching for her but without success. The sea creatures had hidden the mermaid well.

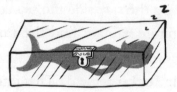

Then one day – ' he lowered his voice to a whisper – 'the ship was boarded by pirates.'

Pirates again?! Atticus scratched his ear. It was all Mr Tucker could talk about!

'The pirate captain made a bargain with the old woman. He agreed to help her find the mermaid if she told him the rhyme. The old woman thought if anyone could find the mermaid, a pirate could, so she did as the pirate captain asked: she told him the rhyme.'

Magic mermaid on the shore, please grant me what I'm wishing for. Atticus said it again in his head.

'Then what happened?' Michael asked.

'What do youze think?!' Mr Tucker chortled. 'As soon as the old goat said the rhyme, the pirate captain made her walk the plank! Then he set sail to find the caarrsket for himself.'

At least the mermaid was safe from the old woman, Atticus thought. But the pirates didn't sound any better. Now the mermaid had to hide from them instead!

'Did the pirate captain find the casket?' Callie asked.

'Nope,' Mr Tucker replied. 'That one didn't, nor

any that came after him: not in almost a thousand years of looking. Some claimed they came close: others told tales of ships being destroyed by the magical sea creatures.' He paused. 'But one thing them sea creatures were wrong about: the rhyme didn't get forgotten, it got passed down through the years from pirate to pirate.'

'So, the Casket of Desires is still out there,' Michael said slowly.

'Aye.' Mr Tucker nodded. 'According to pirate lore.'

'. . . And the person who finds it and summons the mermaid will have their wishes come true,' breathed Callie.

'Aye.' Mr Tucker nodded again. 'That caarrsket falls into the wrong hands and we're all finished. Whoever gets to it first could wish for anything.'

There was silence in the kitchen.

'So where does Fishhook Frank come into it?' Michael asked.

Atticus jumped. He'd been so engrossed in the mermaid story he'd forgotten about Fishhook Frank and the message in the bottle.

Mr Tucker looked uncomfortable. 'Fishhook

and me used to be best friends,' he admitted. 'Many years ago, see, we went lookin' for the caarrsket ourselves. That's when I came across the giant lobster that clipped off me leg. It's one of the creatures that guards the mermaid.'

Atticus could hardly believe his ears. *Mr Tucker had gone in search of the casket?* He wondered if Mrs Tucker knew.

'Does Mrs Tucker know?' Callie asked.

Mr Tucker glowered at her. 'What do youze think?' he said rudely. 'Anyway, after I's lost me leg, I gave up, but Fishhook couldn't rest until he found out where the caarrsket was hidden.' He scratched his beard-jumper in disbelief. 'And now it looks like he has. That's why he's sent this message. He knows if any pirate reads it they'll rescue him like a shot.' Mr Tucker took a deep breath and exhaled noisily. 'The problem is, what happens when they do.'

Atticus rubbed his whiskers with a paw. He was trying to puzzle something out.

Suddenly Mr Tucker banged his fist on the table. 'One thing's certain: we mustn't breathe a word about this when them pirates come for the beard-jumper competition. Or they'll be off to that island before you can say "prawn cocktail". Promise youze won't tell a soul.'

'We promise.' The children nodded solemnly.

Atticus purred distractedly.

'Then once they'ze gone, we'll go and rescue Fishhook ourselves!' Mr Tucker said cheerfully. 'Meanwhile I'll hide this!' He picked up the message and pushed it back into the bottle.

Atticus watched it disappear. He recognised the skull and crossbones emblem on the message now. It was the Jolly Roger: the pirate flag. Atticus felt his fur prickle. No wonder Mr Tucker knew so much about pirates! Atticus had finally figured it out. His suspicions had been right! *Fishhook Frank was a pirate. He and Mr Tucker had been best friends.* That could only mean one thing.

Mr Tucker had once been a pirate too!

'Melons for sale! Melons for sale!'

In Egypt, Jimmy Magpie and his gang were having a horrible time. The three black-and-white birds were each tethered to Zenia Klob's squeaky melon cart by a leather strap around one foot. (Normally Zenia Klob had a squeaky wheelie trolley but since she'd been in hiding she had a squeaky melon cart instead.)

Their magpie mates, Pig, Wally and Gizzard, had escaped when the villains fled from the plague of locusts. But unluckily for Jimmy, Thug and Slasher, Ginger Biscuit had pinned them with his ferocious claws before they could get away.

'Melons for sale! Two for a pound!' Zenia shouted. She was dressed in a djellaba so that the

Egyptian police wouldn't see her. It covered everything from her short wiry grey hair to her big army boots. The only things visible were her black beady eyes and a couple of hairpins that poked out from under her headdress. The hairpins were covered in sleeping potion. They were Zenia's favourite weapon from her days as a Russian KGB agent.

The magpies perched in a line on the rear edge of the cart beside the wall. The cart was parked in a busy market in an even busier town. The market was a labyrinth of narrow streets and twisting alleyways. It had been the magpies' home for the last few months, during which time they'd eaten nothing but melon.

'Lunchtime, birdies!' Zenia chopped one of the melons in half with a big knife and offered it to the magpies. 'Vot vould you like, Biscuit?' she crooned.

Ginger Biscuit was lying on a soft camelskin rug in a basket next to the stall. He yawned and stretched lazily. Then he lifted a paw in the air and popped out his claws one by one – POP. POP. POP. POP. – and pretended to grab at something. 'Rrrrrr,' he said.

'You mean rrrrrrrat,' Zenia Klob said. Ginger Biscuit loved rat. It was his favourite food, except for the stomach, which he spat out. 'I told you, I'm out of rat. You ate the last one yesterday.'

'Myaw!' Ginger Biscuit rolled over so that his back was towards Zenia.

'Don't sulk, my orange angel of darkness,' Zenia sighed. Ginger Biscuit was always grumpy when she ran out of rat. 'I'll get you something else. How about a nice piece of goat?'

Ginger Biscuit twisted his head in Zenia's direction and gave her an evil look.

'Okay, steak then. I'll be back in a minute.' She hurried off.

'CHAKA-CHAKA-CHAKA-CHAKA-CHAKA.' As soon as she had gone the magpies started chattering angrily.

'How come you get steak when all we get is melon?' Slasher complained. Slasher was a thin magpie with a hooked foot. He was even thinner after living on a diet of melon for three months. He sniffed. A delicious smell of food came from some of the other market stalls. His beak watered.

'Because, Slasher, I'm an orange angel of

darkness and you're a brainless bird.' Ginger Biscuit sat up, took off his collar and started dipping the studs in a bottle of Zenia's sleeping potion.

'I hate melon!' Thug moaned. Thug had once been fat with a raggedy tail. Now he was less fat although his tail was more raggedy than ever. 'I want worms.'

'So do I, Thug,' Slasher sighed. 'But you can't have worms, just melon. Not until we get out of here, anyway.'

'And there's not much chance of that!' Ginger Biscuit placed his collar over the back of the basket to dry and lay down again. He laughed. 'Remember what happened the last time you tried to escape?'

Thug and Slasher glanced at one another.

'That was your fault,' Thug said.

'No it wasn't, it was yours!' Slasher protested.

'No, it was yours,' Thug squawked.

Slasher scowled at him. 'It was Jimmy's idea!' The words were out of Slasher's beak before he could stop them.

Thug looked horrified. No one criticised Jimmy, unless they wanted their head pecked.

Jimmy Magpie was tethered the other side of

Thug. He was bigger than the other two magpies and his feathers were glossier. His black tail had a greenish hue and there were flashes of blue in his wings. His eyes glittered. 'What did you say?' he asked coldly.

'Nothing, Boss,' Slasher gulped.

'It's lucky for you, Slasher, I can't quite reach you,' Jimmy said, straining at the strap. 'Or you'd have a hooked beak as well as a hooked foot. That way I could be sure you'd keep it shut.'

'Yes, Boss. Sorry, Boss,' Slasher muttered. He was very glad Jimmy couldn't reach him. Being punched by Jimmy was like flying into a window: you didn't see it coming and it hurt a lot.

'Well, whoever's idea it was to try and escape by hiding inside the melons, you've got to admit it was pretty dumb!' Ginger Biscuit chortled. 'I thought I'd never stop laughing when Zenia sliced one open and nearly chopped Thug's head off!'

'Yeah, ha ha!' Thug said bitterly. 'Very funny, I'm sure.'

'And the state of your feathers!' Ginger Biscuit sniggered. 'Who'd have thought melon juice was so sticky? You looked like you'd been swimming in snot.'

41

'Tell him to stop making fun of us, Boss,' Thug said plaintively. 'It's snot fair.'

Jimmy's glittering eyes moved over Ginger Biscuit with contempt. 'You're beginning to remind me a lot of Atticus Claw,' he said quietly. 'The way you lie about, sneering.'

Ginger Biscuit got up. 'I'm nothing like Claw,' he snarled. 'He's a traitor: a disgrace to cat burgling.' His eyes narrowed. 'He thinks he's better than us now he's a police cat. He thinks he's cool just cos he's got a shiny badge and stopped us raiding a tomb full of treasure. Well he's not!' Ginger Biscuit bared his teeth. 'Next time I see him, he's dead.'

Jimmy Magpie blinked. 'That's what you said when he stopped us stealing the crown jewels,' he remarked. 'And it didn't turn out too well then.'

'Next time will be different,' Ginger Biscuit growled. 'Wait and see. Instead of a camel rug I'll have a cat one. And I'll use that handkerchief of his to spit rat guts into.'

'Not so fast, Ginger-chops,' Thug said. 'We've got a few plans of our own for Atticus Claw when we get back to Littleton-on-Sea.'

'CHAKA-CHAKA-CHAKA-CHAKA-CHAKA!'

The magpies chattered excitedly. The thought of Littleton-on-Sea cheered them. But not as much as the thought of what they planned to do to Atticus Claw when they arrived. Thinking up horrible ways to get their revenge was how Thug and Slasher made it through the day.

'We're gonna get the crows in to beak him up,' Thug boasted.

'Then the jackdaws are gonna drop a brick on his head,' Slasher explained.

'Then the jays are gonna pull out his claws so that Jimmy can make them into a knuckleduster,' Thug chuckled.

'Then we'll use his tail to patch up the nest,' Slasher sniggered.

'And we'll make the rest of him into a nest snuggler,' Thug finished.

'Sure. But first you've got to get out of here,' Ginger Biscuit yawned. 'And I've already told you, there's not much chance of that.'

'What does Zenia want to keep us for anyway?' Slasher grumbled. 'She doesn't need us any more.'

43

'Because she doesn't want you singing your heads off to the fuzz,' Ginger told him. 'Anyway, you go back to Littleton-on-Sea and Inspector Cheddar will arrest you again.'

'I hate that bloke,' Thug grumbled.

'And his cheesy kids,' Slasher spat.

'You'll end up back in Her Majesty's Prison for Bad Birds.'

Slasher pulled a face. 'That place was torture!'

'It was better than this,' Thug said gloomily. 'At least we didn't have to clean out Zenia's poo bucket. Only Jimmy's.'

'Here ve are!' Zenia returned with a plateful of chopped steak. She placed it in front of Ginger Biscuit.

Just then two men approached the stall. One had no teeth. The other had no hair. They both wore eye patches. One of the men wore a long blue velvet jacket with lace at the sleeves.

'Look at the buttons on that!' Thug regarded them longingly. 'They're all shiny.'

'Ahoy there, matey!' the one with no teeth said.

Zenia Klob rounded on them. 'It's Ms, not matey!' she screeched. 'Vot do you vant? I got

44

melons, two for an Egyptian pound.'

'How about three for a doubloon?' One of the men produced a gold coin from his pocket.

Zenia snatched it and raised it to the light to get a better look. 'Vere did you get this?' she demanded greedily.

The man snatched it back. 'Never you mind. We don't want any melon anyway. We want your parrots.'

'What parrots?' Thug looked about.

'I think he means us,' Jimmy Magpie said. His eyes gleamed. 'Quick boys, start squawking!'

'Why?' Slasher whispered.

'Cos this might be our ticket out of here!' Jimmy hissed. 'These clowns think we're parrots! Zenia wants their money. If she sells us, we can escape!'

'Oh yeah!' Thug said. 'That's brilliant, that is, Jimmy.'

'Squawk, squawk!' the magpies cried. 'Squawk, squawk!'

'Shut it, birdies,' Zenia Klob cried. 'Or I'll hairpin you!'

The magpies fell silent.

'How much?' the man with the jacket asked.

'Thirty doubloons for a pair,' Zenia said.

'Ten,' the man countered.

'Tventy,' Zenia came back.

The man hesitated. 'What do you think, Tony?' he asked his friend. 'This one looks pretty mangy.' He prodded Thug with a fat finger.

'Who are you calling mangy?' Thug cried. 'Chaka-chaka-chaka-chaka-chaka! Oomph!'

Jimmy punched Thug in the crop. 'Don't blow our cover!' he hissed. 'Or you're on poo bucket duty for the rest of the year. Keep squawking!'

'Pam wanted three,' the other man replied.

'Who's Pam?' Slasher whispered.

'A little girl, I should think,' Jimmy said. 'That's why they're buying us. As a gift. For a little girl! How cute! I can't wait to make her miserable by escaping.' He put on a baby voice. 'Boo hoo. Where are my parrots, Daddy?' His voice changed back to normal. 'Oh guess what, they've gone!'

'You're really mean, Boss!' Thug said admiringly.

'Yeah, you're the worst!' Slasher agreed.

'Thanks!' Jimmy looked pleased.

'Squawk! Squawk!'

'Squawk! Squawk!'

'Tell you vot,' Zenia said. She undid the magpies' straps and held them up by the feet. 'You can have the mangy one for free.'

'I'm getting dizzy!' Thug dangled upside down with Jimmy and Slasher. 'All the blood's rushing to my brain.'

'You don't have a brain,' Jimmy told him.

'Done!' the man said. He handed the money over. His eye fell on Ginger Biscuit. 'I don't suppose you'd consider selling your cat, would you?'

'Never!' Zenia Klob shrieked. 'He's not for sale!' She shoved Jimmy, Thug and Slasher into a wicker cage and banged the door shut. 'Especially not to pirates.' She handed the cage to Tony.

Thug and Slasher looked at one another, aghast.

'Did she say what I think she said?' Thug gulped.

'Pirates!' Ginger Biscuit guffawed. 'Nice work, guys! Have fun!'

'Chaka-chaka-chaka-chaka!'

The pirates walked off, swinging the cage.

Zenia Klob waited until they rounded a corner. 'Qvik!' she said. 'Get after them, Biscuit. See vere they go.' Her eyes gleamed. 'Pirates!' she chuckled, 'I've got a feeling they vill lead us to some treasure.'

A few days later, in the ballroom at Toffly Hall, Atticus was watching the final stages of the World Beard-Jumper Competition with Michael and Callie. So far, to Atticus's relief, there hadn't been 'any trouble'. None of the grown-ups (apart from Mr Tucker, of course), had spotted that the people dressed as pirates really *were* pirates. And the pirates hadn't done anything bad, at least nothing that Atticus was aware of anyway. Even so, Atticus couldn't wait for the competition to finish. He still wasn't sure if he'd made the right decision not to let the children tell Inspector Cheddar.

'Ah, Atticus,' Inspector Cheddar strode up. 'There you are. We seem to have lost a few silver teaspoons, I wondered if you knew what had happened to them?'

Atticus pretended not to have heard. The pirates must have stolen them! He felt terrible. If Inspector Cheddar found out the truth, he'd take away his police-cat sergeant badge. And Callie and Michael would get into trouble too.

Two of the pirates barged past. One of them had a wooden leg like Mr Tucker, with raggedy trousers cut off at the knee. The other one had a handkerchief tied round his head decorated with the Jolly Roger, and no shoes. Both had long, straggly beard-jumpers.

'Dear oh dear!' Inspector Cheddar chuckled. 'I've never seen such smelly old costumes. Most of them look like they haven't been washed for years. If I'd hired that for a fancy-dress party I'd want my money back. I must ask them which shop they went to and report it to Trading Standards.' He started after them.

Oh no! Atticus looked desperately at the children. *Now what were they going to do?*

Just then Mr Tucker waved frantically in their direction.

'Dad, it's time for the prize-giving,' Michael ran after Inspector Cheddar and pulled his sleeve. 'The judges are ready. They need you on stage!' Mr Tucker had asked Inspector Cheddar to give out the prizes, mainly to keep him out of the way so he didn't decide to do some detective work amongst the guests.

Atticus breathed a sigh of relief. *Just in time!*

'Okay,' Inspector Cheddar straightened his cap. 'I'll see you later. Atticus, keep an eye on the forks.' He made his way towards the stage to join Mr Tucker, Mrs Tucker, Mrs Cheddar and the judges.

Atticus glanced at the clock. It was half past five. The competition was supposed to finish by six. *Half an hour to go*. He sighed. If at that moment he'd been able to summon the mermaid from the Casket of Desires, he would have wished for it to be six o'clock already so that nothing went wrong!

The Casket of Desires. That was another thing worrying Atticus. *What if the pirates found out about Fishhook Frank's message?* Mr Tucker said he'd hidden it in a safe place but was anywhere safe when your house was full of pirates? Atticus wasn't sure. And he wasn't sure about Mr Tucker's plan to rescue Fishhook Frank either. The plan, if you could call it that, was to tell Inspector Cheddar and Mrs Tucker all about the message in the bottle when the beard-jumper competition was over, then set sail to rescue Frank and get to him before a pirate did. It sounded simple enough but Mrs Tucker would hit the roof if she found out that Mr Tucker had once been a pirate. Not to mention the fact that Atticus had never been sailing before or that they didn't even know where Fishhook Frank was. So it wasn't simple at all! Sometimes Atticus couldn't help thinking life had been a lot easier when he was a cat burglar.

'Don't worry, Atticus,' Callie whispered kindly.

'It'll be okay as long as the pirates don't steal any more cutlery.' Michael gave him a stroke.

Atticus wished he felt so confident about it. He had a bad feeling that something was about to happen. His instinct was kicking in again.

'And now for the moment youze all been waiting for,' Mr Tucker took to the stage. 'The judges have made their decision.' He nodded towards the back of the stage. The judges sat behind a table with the prizes on it. Mrs Tucker and Mrs Cheddar sat beside them. 'Please welcome Inspector Ian Cheddar who will announce the winners of this year's World Beard-Jumper Competition.' There was a round of applause from the hall. Some of the pirates took the stolen teaspoons out of their pockets and banged them on their hooks.

Atticus saw Mrs Tucker's forehead crinkle into a frown. Her eyes scanned the room. Mrs Tucker used to be a secret agent called Agent Whelk. She was very good at finding things out. Her eyes met Atticus's. Atticus felt himself blush under his fur. Mrs Tucker was also very good at knowing when he was being naughty. He looked away.

Mr Tucker raised his hands for quiet. 'And then my lovely wife, Edna, will hand out the prizes for the best-dressed pirate . . . er . . . I mean, the best pirate *costume!*' Mrs Tucker gave her husband a sharp glance. Mr Tucker shifted uncomfortably. So did Atticus. *She definitely suspected something!*

'So, without further ado, I'll hand over to

Inspector Cheddar.' Mr Tucker shuffled behind the table to join the others.

Inspector Cheddar climbed the steps to the stage and stood in front of the microphone. He had a gold envelope in his hand.

'Good afternoon, ladies, gentlemen, children, fishermen . . .' he sniggered '. . . and – er – *pirates*!'

There was silence in the hall.

Inspector Cheddar ripped open the envelope. 'In third place, we have Hairy Mac. Come on up, Mac, there's a bottle of Thumpers' Traditional Beard Dye for you!'

Hairy Mac was one of Mr Tucker's fishermen friends. Like the rest of the fishermen his beard-jumper was tucked into a pair of brightly coloured waterproof dungarees, which in turn were tucked into a pair of brightly coloured rubber boots. There was a smattering of applause as Hairy Mac went to collect his prize. Some of the pirates booed.

'In second place, we have Short John Silver. Where are you, John?' Inspector Cheddar peered out across the sea of bristly faces. 'Ah, there you are!' A tiny pirate in a dirty coat pushed his way through the crowds. His beard-jumper brushed the floor. He had to pick it up in his arms to stop himself tripping over it.

'Impressive!' Inspector Cheddar remarked. He bent down to give Short John Silver his prize. 'A box set of 'Thumpers' Traditional Beard Wax.'

Short John Silver hobbled off to whistles of approval from the pirates.

'And in first place we have . . .' Inspector Cheddar paused.

The crowd fell silent.

'. . . our very own Mr Herman Tucker!'

The fishermen cheered. So did the pirates.

Atticus thought he knew why that was. It was because Mr Tucker had been a fisherman *and* a pirate. He wondered if Mrs Tucker had noticed anything strange about it. He didn't dare look at her.

'Well done, Mr Tucker!' The children shouted. Atticus purred weakly. He was pleased for Mr Tucker but all he really cared about was getting to home time. He glanced at the clock. *Nearly six.* *Thank goodness!*

Mr Tucker limped across the stage to accept his prize. It was a deluxe spa day at Thumpers' Traditional Beard Spa. He beamed with pride.

'Congratulations, Mr Tucker!' Inspector Cheddar led the final round of applause. 'And now I'd like to hand over to Mrs Tucker to give out the fancy-dress prizes.' He stepped away from the microphone.

Suddenly there was a terrible roar from the back of the ballroom. 'Not so fast, you scurvy landlubbers!'

Atticus looked round.

A huge man dressed all in black stood at the entrance to the ballroom. He wore a long coat, breeches and boots that pulled up over his knees. Beneath his three-pointed hat a mass of curly black hair had been swept into a ponytail. Over one eye he wore an eye patch. But the most striking thing about the newcomer was his beard-jumper. It tumbled around his chin in a thick tangle of wool and bristle so that it appeared as if his very jumper had been knitted from his whiskers (or the other way around).

Atticus stared at him in horror. It had to be him:

the only pirate Mr Tucker hadn't sent an invitation to, the only one who would cause trouble if he turned up uninvited, which he just had.

It was Captain Black Beard-Jumper!

Captain Black Beard-Jumper strode across the ballroom floor towards the stage. The sound of his boots rang around the room like thunderclaps. His face was contorted into an ugly scowl.

The crowd parted in front of him to let him through. Some of the pirates removed their hats and bowed with a flourish as he passed.

Atticus found himself in Callie's arms. He must have jumped up there without realising. It made him feel a lot safer. He wondered what would happen next.

Captain Black Beard-Jumper leapt on to the stage. He gave another great roar. 'Think you could hold the World Beard-Jumper Competition without telling me, did you, you bunch of lily-livered sea-dogs?'

Mr Tucker had retreated to the back of the stage. He pulled Mrs Cheddar and the judges under the table. Only Mrs Tucker remained in her place. She had her hands on her hips and was glaring at Mr Tucker. *If she didn't know there was something fishy going on before,* Atticus thought resignedly, *she definitely knows now.*

Inspector Cheddar stared at the pirate in astonishment. 'Who are you?' he said.

'Who am I, you say? WHO AM I? I'll tell you who I am,' the pirate roared. 'I'm Captain Black Beard-Jumper, first pirate of the Seven Seas. Owner of the biggest beard-jumper known to chins.'

Inspector Cheddar looked nonplussed. Then, to Atticus's amazement, he started to laugh. 'Oh, I get it,' he said. 'Mr Tucker hired you. You're part of the entertainment.'

'Dad thinks he's in fancy dress!' Michael whispered. 'He doesn't realise he's a real pirate!'

'What are we going to do?' Callie squeaked. 'Atticus, think of something! We've got to help Dad!'

Atticus screwed up his eyes and tried to concentrate. But the only thing he could think of was that he wished he hadn't listened to Mr Tucker. The children had been right about the pirates. They should have told Inspector Cheddar.

'Ooh aarr!' Inspector Cheddar shouted. 'Shiver me timbers! Yo ho ho and a bottle of rum!'

'Are you takin' the mick out of me, you hornswaggling squiffy?' Captain Black Beard-Jumper hissed.

'Oh, this is priceless!' Inspector Cheddar doubled over with mirth. 'Come on, Mrs Tucker, give the man his prize for the best pirate costume. He deserves it. He even had *me* fooled for a minute.'

Black Beard-Jumper's eyes narrowed. 'This be no costume, you scallywag. Now get out of my way before I have you flogged. It's Tucker I want.'

'Very good!' Inspector Cheddar sniggered. To Atticus's horror he reached up and gave Captain Black Beard-Jumper's ponytail a tug. 'You even glued on your wig!'

There was a gasp from the pirates. The fishermen made for the exit.

'Wig, you say? How dare you!' Black Beard-Jumper thundered. 'I'll have your guts for garters.'

'Ha ha ha!' Inspector Cheddar wiped tears of laughter from his eyes. 'I'll bet you've even got a glass eye!' He pinged Black Beard-Jumper's eye patch. 'I knew it!'

Captain Black Beard-Jumper drew his sword from its scabbard and pointed it at Inspector Cheddar.

Atticus covered his eyes with his paws.

'Wait!' Mr Tucker crawled out from under the table.

'Tucker!' Black Beard-Jumper hissed. 'Try and steal the prize for the biggest beard-jumper from me, would you? Like you once stole my ship's cat?'

Atticus's ears pricked up. *Mr Tucker had once stolen Black Beard-Jumper's ship's cat? No wonder there was bad blood between them.*

'That was a long time ago,' Mr Tucker retorted. 'And Bones didn't like you anyway. She was glad to come away with me and Fishhook.'

Bones? Atticus had heard of Bones before, although he had never met her. According to Mr Tucker, Bones had saved his life on more than one occasion at sea.

Atticus wasn't the only one who had heard of Bones. Mrs Tucker pursed her lips. It was obvious to Atticus she was beginning to work things out.

'Rubbish!' Captain Black Beard-Jumper shouted. 'Bones was always loyal to her captain.'

'It be the pirate code!' Inspector Cheddar said in a silly voice. 'That a ship's cat be loyal to its captain, it do. Ooh aarr.'

Black Beard-Jumper snarled. He turned on Inspector Cheddar and drew back his sword. 'That's enough lip from you, matey!' he yelled. 'Now prepare to die.'

Atticus could hardly bear to watch.

'Youze run him through with your sword, Black Beard-Jumper, and youze'll have me to answer to,' Mr Tucker shouted.

'You'll have to do better than that, Tucker.' Captain Black Beard-Jumper's grip tightened on the hilt of his sword. 'Give me one reason why I shouldn't.'

'It's a double act!' Inspector Cheddar hooted. 'Brilliant!'

Mr Tucker hesitated.

'Well, Tucker . . . ?' Captain Black Beard-Jumper said. 'I'm waiting.'

'Okay, youze wins!' Mr Tucker sat back with a bump. He started to unscrew his wooden leg.

Callie's arms tightened around Atticus's tummy. 'What's he doing?'

'I don't know,' Michael stood frozen with fear.

Atticus thought he did. There was only one thing that would stop Captain Black Beard-Jumper running Inspector Cheddar through with his sword. And that thing was Fishhook Frank's message in a bottle. It must be hidden inside Mr Tucker's wooden leg!

Atticus watched closely as Mr Tucker upended his leg and gave it a shake. He was right! It was hollow! The message in a bottle rolled on to the stage. Mr Tucker picked it up. He grasped the leg with his free hand and waved it at the Captain. 'It's from Fishhook Frank,' he said. 'He's found out where the caarrsket is hidden. You find Fishhook, Black Beard-Jumper, and he'll take you to it. That's what you want, isn't it?'

Low muttering rippled around the ballroom. All the pirates knew what that meant.

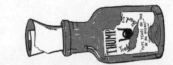

'A casket!' Inspector Cheddar yelled in his pretend pirate voice. 'Of treasure, I'll be bound! Ooh aarr!'

'Give me the bottle,' Captain Black Beard-Jumper demanded.

'Not unless you put your sword away,' Mr Tucker said. 'Or I'll smash it to bits and grind the paper into dust. That way youze'll never find Fishhook. Or the caarrsket.' He held the bottle by the stopper against the floor and raised his wooden leg ready to smash it into smithereens.

'Stop!' Captain Black Beard-Jumper shouted. 'All right. Have it your way, Tucker. I promise I won't kill the bilge rat.' He replaced the sword in its scabbard and held out his hand. 'If you give me the bottle.'

'Phew!' Inspector Cheddar giggled. 'You had me worried there for a minute. Not!!'

'Throw it over,' Captain Black Beard-Jumper ordered.

Mr Tucker tossed the bottle towards him.

The pirate captain caught it. He held it up and twisted it to and fro between his finger and thumb, examining its contents. 'The Casket of Desires!'

He grinned. 'I wonder what I'll wish for first. Pirate King of the world? Death to everyone who ain't a pirate?' He pocketed his prize and turned back to Inspector Cheddar. 'That reminds me.' Suddenly his big hairy hand shot out and grabbed Inspector Cheddar by the throat.

Inspector Cheddar's eyes popped. 'That's taking it a bit far!' he croaked.

'You promised not to kill him!' Callie screamed. She put Atticus down and rushed towards the stage.

Atticus rushed after her.

'I'm not going to kill him,' Black Beard-Jumper said, without looking away from Inspector Cheddar's face. 'I'm going to curse him.'

At the mention of the word curse, the pirates stampeded towards the door. They pushed and shoved their way out.

'Okay, show's over!' Inspector Cheddar gasped. 'Time to go home!'

Callie clambered on to the stage. Atticus leapt up behind her. He had to protect Callie from Black Beard-Jumper, whatever happened.

'Callie!' Mrs Cheddar screeched. 'No!'

'Stay away, Callie!' Mr Tucker shouted, trying to stand up on his good leg 'Edna! Do something!'

Mrs Tucker had already left her chair. She had a determined look on her face. Atticus could see from her expression that she knew this was for real.

'Sorry, Callie, but you're not going near that pirate.' Mrs Tucker grabbed Callie. She sidestepped Captain Black Beard-Jumper and pushed Callie towards her mum. Mrs Cheddar pulled Callie under the table and hugged her. Mrs Tucker dropped to her hands and knees.

Atticus ran towards Black Beard-Jumper, snarling. Callie might be safe but he still had to do something to help Inspector Cheddar.

Captain Black Beard-Jumper pulled back a boot and aimed a kick in his direction.

Atticus dodged. The boot whistled past his whiskers. He turned round, ready for another charge.

'No, Atticus.' Atticus felt Mrs Tucker grab him by the scruff of the neck and bundle him up. She shuffled back to the table on her knees and held him close. 'There's nothing you can do,' she whispered. 'It's too late.'

Captain Black Beard-Jumper drew Inspector Cheddar towards him so that their eyes were level. 'By the power invested in me as the greatest pirate on the Seven Seas with the biggest beard-jumper known to chins,' he hissed, 'I hereby mark you for death on the thirteenth day of the seventh month at sunset.' He dropped Inspector Cheddar and nudged him with his boot. 'That'll teach you to pull my ponytail.' He leapt off the stage and strode out of the hall.

Atticus listened as the echo of the Captain's boots receded down the passageway.

The front door banged.

There was silence. Everyone had gone, except the Cheddars, the Tuckers and Atticus.

Mr Tucker started to crawl towards the steps that led down from the stage.

'Where do you think you're going?' Mrs Tucker stood over him. 'Well, Herman? What do you have to say for yourself? You've got a lot of explaining to do.'

Atticus sat in a big leather chair in the Police Commissioner's enormous office at Scotland Yard. All four Cheddars were there. So were Mr and Mrs Tucker. Atticus felt miserable. No one had paid him any attention in the car on the way there from Littleton-on-Sea. In fact no one had paid him any attention at all since the disastrous events at Toffly Hall. There had been no sardines. And the only cat food left in the cupboard at home was a box of dried pellets that tasted like cardboard and smelt like mummified rabbit poo. They were all too worried about Inspector Cheddar to think about him.

Atticus couldn't blame them. He was worried too.

'Bad business this, Cheddar,' the Police Commissioner said.

'Yes, sir.' Inspector Cheddar looked dazed.

'I should tell you that the PM and the Queen have both asked to be kept informed,' the Police Commissioner said.

Atticus felt even more miserable. *The Queen knew about this?!* Her Majesty used to be his friend. He couldn't imagine that she would be very impressed with him now.

'Any sign of the black spot, Cheddar?' the Police Commissioner enquired sympathetically.

'No, not yet.' Inspector Cheddar examined his hands. 'Although I do have a verruca on my right foot. I think I got it when I took the children swimming.'

There was a knock at the door.

A tall man in a smart uniform came in.

'This is Commander Whale,' the Police Commissioner introduced him. 'From the Royal Navy. I believe he has news for us.'

'Captain Black Beard-Jumper's ship, the *Golden Doubloon*, was sighted a couple of days ago heading towards a group of islands off the coast of

Indonesia called the Moluccas,' the
Commander said. 'Unfortunately my men
lost him. The waters around there are
extremely treacherous for naval vessels. Our ships
are too big. There's only one way to get close to
some of those islands. And that's with an old-
fashioned sailing boat.'

'Thank you, Commander.' The Police
Commissioner turned to Mr Tucker. 'Mr Tucker,'
he said gravely, 'I understand from your wife Agent
Whelk that you used to be a pirate.'

'Aye,' Mr Tucker said tersely.

Mrs Tucker had forced the whole story out of
him. It turned out that both he and Fishhook Frank
had once sailed with Captain Black Beard-Jumper
on his pirate ship, the *Golden Doubloon*.

'And that you know this Fishhook Frank fellow.'

'Aye!'

'And that it was originally your idea not to
inform the authorities that Toffly Hall would be
seething with pirates during the World Beard-
Jumper Competition.'

'Aye!!'

'And that if we don't get to the Casket of Desires

before Captain Black Beard-Jumper does, then we face possible world domination by pirates.'

'All right, don't rub it in!' Mr Tucker grumbled.

'Serves you right!' Mrs Tucker muttered. 'You should have told me about those pirates in the first place.'

'It was Atticus,' Mr Tucker protested. 'He was fine with it! You ask the children.'

What? Atticus was startled. *He wasn't fine with it! He just didn't know what to do. He'd never had to make an important police-catting decision like that on his own before.* He hoped that wasn't what Michael and Callie thought.

'And on top of that,' the Police Commissioner went on, 'Inspector Cheddar has been cursed with the mark of the black spot which basically means he's going to die in . . .' The Police Commissioner consulted his calendar . . . 'eight days. That's your fault too, right?'

'AYE!' Mr Tucker exploded.

'There must be a cure for the curse,' Mrs Cheddar said bravely. 'Isn't there?' She held the children's hands tightly.

'Well, Herman, is there? You're the expert!' Mrs

Tucker snapped. 'You're the one who knows all about pirate lore.'

Mr Tucker looked sheepish 'There's only one way to lift the curse,' he said eventually. 'And that's for us to find the caarrsket and for Inspector Cheddar to summon the mermaid and make a wish.'

'What happens if we can't find it?' It was Inspector Cheddar who spoke. 'Only I wouldn't mind knowing, as it's my life on the line. If that's all right with *you*, Atticus,' he added bitterly.

Atticus's ears drooped. *Inspector Cheddar blamed him too!*

'First youze get the sweats,' Mr Tucker said gloomily. 'Then youze get the scabs. After that youze get the sickness, then youze get the squirts. Then comes the scratchin', the lumps, the bumps and the camel humps. After that your hair drops out and your eyes combust. Then . . .'

'Shut up, Herman!' Mrs Tucker said. 'You're upsetting the children.' She leaned forward. 'It seems to me there's only one thing to do. We've got to find that casket before Black Beard-Jumper does.'

71

'That's what I's been saying all along!' Mr Tucker protested. 'Haven't I, Atticus?'

Atticus ignored him. Mr Tucker couldn't tell tales on him one minute and be nice to him the next.

'I agree,' the Police Commissioner said. 'And fortunately for you, Inspector Cheddar, Mr Tucker, with his pirating experience, is uniquely placed to help us.'

'Hooray!' said Inspector Cheddar sarcastically. 'Lucky me!'

'Look, I's sorry for what happened,' Mr Tucker mumbled. 'But the Police Commissioner's right. I can help. I think I knows where Fishhook be marooned. There was a map on the back of the message.'

Atticus recalled the mass of squiggly lines and jumbled numbers. He remembered thinking at the time that if anyone knew what it meant, Mr Tucker would.

'I's been there with Frank, see?' Mr Tucker continued. 'When we was lookin' for the caarrsket the laarrst time around: that's where we camped before we started our voyage. Fishhook must have gone looking for the caarrsket again, then got himself into trouble and ended up marooned back there.'

'Well that's a start,' the Police Commissioner said. 'Commander?'

'We can have a ship ready in one of the Moluccan ports in a day or so,' the Commander said. 'Mr Tucker just needs to put together a crew.' He turned to Mr Tucker. 'The Navy will fly you out there. If you're quick, you might still beat Black Beard-Jumper to the island to rescue Fishhook Frank. It's possible he may be able to lead you to the casket. What happens after that . . .' he shrugged . . . 'I can't say.'

There was silence in the room. Atticus was thinking about Mr Tucker's story; about the poor hunted mermaid; about the legendary sea creatures that guarded her; and about what happened to Mr Tucker's leg when he went in search of the casket the first time. Even supposing they did get to the casket before Black Beard-Jumper did, would they be able to save Inspector Cheddar? What if the mermaid didn't wake up? What if she had gone? What if they didn't get there in time? Inspector Cheddar only had eight days to live.

The Police Commissioner nodded. 'Mr Tucker, do you have a crew in mind?'

'Aye.' Mr Tucker pulled a list from his pocket.

Captain	Mr Tucker
First Mate	Mrs Tucker
First Aider	Mrs Cheddar
Cursed Sailor	Inspector Cheddar
Deck Hands	Callie and Michael
Ship's Cat	Atticus

'Very well,' the Police Commissioner agreed. 'Good luck, everyone. The future of the world as we know it depends on you. Not to mention Inspector Cheddar's life.'

'Okay, okay!' Mr Tucker was still grumbling. 'No need to go on about it!'

Atticus shuffled out after the others. *Ship's cat?* He hated water. He didn't know anything about ships. How was he ever going to make a good ship's cat? He almost wished he wasn't going.

'I came to say goodbye.' Later that evening he met Mimi beside the beach huts.

'You mean au revoir,' Mimi said.

'What's the difference?' Atticus knew a little bit of French from when he'd lived in Monte Carlo. But he couldn't see what it had to do with anything now.

'Au revoir means "until we meet again",' Mimi explained gently. 'It's not as final as goodbye.'

'Look, Mimi,' Atticus said suddenly, 'I'm not sure I will be back this time.'

Mimi's golden eyes bored into him. 'What do you mean?'

'It's the Cheddars,' Atticus said heavily. 'Callie and Michael wanted to tell their dad about the pirates, but they didn't because of me. They thought I'd know what to do because I'm a police cat. Only I didn't: I got it wrong. And I'm worried they won't love me any more because of what's happened. I mean, Inspector Cheddar never did love me,' he added, 'but now he thinks him being cursed is my fault.' He reached for Mimi's paw. 'What if Mrs Cheddar thinks that too?' he said helplessly. 'And Callie and Michael? Even if I *can*

75

help them find the mermaid, they might never forgive me for not letting Inspector Cheddar know about the pirates. They might not want me around afterwards.'

Mimi squeezed his paw. 'Atticus, don't say things like that! Mrs Cheddar and the children do love you. They're worried. That's all. Everything will be all right once you find the casket.'

'But I've let them down,' Atticus insisted. 'If only I hadn't listened to Mr Tucker then none of this would have happened.'

'That's called the benefit of hindsight,' Mimi said.

Atticus looked at her questioningly.

'Hindsight is when you look back on things and wish you'd done them differently,' she explained. 'Everyone has it.'

'Do they?' Atticus asked.

'Of course!' Mimi let go of his paw. She held his gaze. 'Listen, Atticus, everyone makes mistakes all the time. The most important thing is that you learn from them.'

'Maybe you're right . . .' Atticus felt a bit brighter. Mimi always gave him good advice when he needed it. 'I wish you were coming with me,' he sighed.

'Me too!' Mimi giggled. 'Our last adventure was so much fun. But I can't be away from Aysha that long. Her baby's due any day now.' Aysha was Mimi's owner. She had a flower shop in Littleton-on-Sea.

'Don't you mind?' Atticus said. 'About the baby? I think I might be a bit jealous if I were you.' He laughed. 'I was even cross when Mr Tucker gave Thomas an extra sardine for finding the message in the bottle! I mean, how silly is that?!'

'Very.' Mimi laughed too. 'I can't wait for the baby. It'll be fun to have someone to play with. I've always wanted to be around children. You're so lucky having Callie and Michael.' She got up, ready for their evening stroll. 'Now trust me. Everything will be fine.'

Atticus followed her on to the beach. He was lucky. He knew that. Which was why he'd do anything he could to help the Cheddars. He decided not to say anything else to Mimi about how dangerous the voyage was; about how scared he was of the sea. He didn't want to spoil their evening. But deep down he still wondered if it would be the last one they ever spent together.

On board the *Golden Doubloon*, the magpies were scrubbing seagull poop off the poop deck. More precisely Thug and Slasher were scrubbing seagull poop off the poop deck. Jimmy was up on the mainsail talking to Pam.

Pam, it turned out, wasn't a little girl. She was Captain Black Beard-Jumper's parrot: and she was mean, like the Captain. That's why she liked Jimmy. And Jimmy liked her. Or at least he pretended he did. Pam had something he wanted: information. Jimmy had been eavesdropping: the word amongst the crew was that the Captain was going after treasure. There were rumours of a precious casket. And Jimmy was determined to find out what was in it.

'Did I tell you about the time I stole a tiara, Pamela?' Jimmy bragged. 'It was so cool. I made this speech, right. There were thousands of birds there. All hanging on my every word . . .'

Thug and Slasher were listening to the conversation.

'Yeah, and then you got arrested,' Slasher muttered. 'By Claw.' He pushed a filthy sponge around the deck with his hooked foot.

The two magpies were chained to a bucket. Not that they could have escaped. They were surrounded by sea. They hadn't had sight of land for days. They had absolutely no clue where they were.

Pam didn't hear Slasher. 'Nice one, Jim!' she squawked. 'You're the kind of bird who can get on in life, especially on a pirate ship. Even though you're not a parrot.'

'I hate parrots,' Thug murmured. 'They're worse than melons.' Pam had tied his tail to a mop with a bit of rope. He sloshed about in the poop, trying not to trip over. 'Chaka-chaka-chaka-chaka-chaka!'

'I've told you, Pamela,' Jimmy said, 'magpies

are just as good as parrots. We're nasty. We're cruel. We're clever.' He paused. 'And we like treasure.'

'That's true, Thug,' Slasher said. 'You've got to admit the Boss is right about that.'

'Yeah, I like a bit of treasure,' Thug nodded. 'Especially glittery things. Not much sign of it round here, though,' he added bitterly. He poked at a sticky seagull dropping with the mop. ''Ere, Slash, pass the Scrubbit, will you?'

Slasher pushed a pack of soap powder towards him.

THUMPERS'
SCRUBBIT

for all your deck cleaning needs
No need to soak!
works on even the toughest droppings

Thug dunked the mop in it and swept it from side to side with his tail. The seagull dropping dissolved into a gloopy soup.

'Magpies can't talk human though, like parrots can,' Pam said dubiously. 'I mean, I like you, Jim, don't get me wrong. But I don't know what the Captain will say when he sees you and realises Toothless Tony bought the wrong birds.'

Captain Black Beard-Jumper had been holed up in his cabin since he rejoined the ship. The magpies had only glimpsed the Captain once, through the cabin window. Captain Black Beard-Jumper had been sitting at a desk with Pam on his shoulder and a small black cat on his knee, surrounded by charts, muttering to himself. He was squinting at a scrap of paper, which he pulled from a bottle with a thin dagger.

'The Captain will love me, Pam,' Jimmy boasted. 'Don't worry.' He sidled towards Pam and put a protective wing around her shoulder. Jimmy cleared his throat. It was time to find out about the treasure. 'So,' he said nonchalantly, 'what's this I hear about a casket?'

'I can't really say, Jim,' Pam said. 'It's a secret.'

Down below on the poop deck, Thug and Slasher stopped scrubbing.

'Did she say "secret"?' Thug whispered.

The magpies loved secrets.

'Yeah!' Slasher whispered back. 'Shhh. Let's listen.'

'You know all the Captain's secrets, don't you, Pam?' Jimmy asked slyly.

'I suppose I do, Jim. He talks to me,' Pam said proudly. 'He says I'm his only real friend. He says if he tells the other pirates things they'll cut his throat and steal everything.'

'It must be hard, having all that responsibility,' Jimmy said. He frowned as if he were thinking something over. 'You're *his* friend, Pam,' he said eventually, 'but what about *you*?'

'What do you mean?' Pam blinked.

'What you need, Pamela, is a friend of your own,' Jimmy said. 'It's lonely out here at sea. You need someone you can share things with.' He snuggled closer to Pam. 'A bird you can trust.' He paused. '*Me*, for instance.'

'He's trying to get her to tell him the secret!' Slasher said excitedly.

'That's clever, that is,' Thug remarked in awe. 'No wonder he's the boss.'

'I'd like to tell you, Jim, I really would . . .' Pam wavered. 'But . . .'

'What's the downside, Pamela?' Jimmy wheedled. 'You said it yourself. I can't talk to humans. I can't tell anyone what you tell me and the Captain's never gonna find out unless *you* tell him.'

'Well, when you put it like that, Jim . . .' Pam put her beak to his ear and started to whisper.

'She's telling him!' Thug and Slasher hopped up and down.

Slasher fell over the mop.

Thug tripped over the sponge.

They ended up in a heap, covered in slimy poop.

'There, so now you know.' Pam stopped whispering. 'Promise you won't tell, Jim?' she begged.

Jimmy's eyes gleamed. Pam's information was better than anything he could have hoped for. He gave her a little pat and removed his wing from her shoulder.

'Of course I won't, Pamela,' he said solemnly. 'It's *our* secret now!'

'I'd better get off and see if the Captain wants anything,' Pam said. She sidled to the edge of the boom and lifted her tail feathers.

SPLAT!

The first dropping landed on Thug's head.

PLOP!

The second one landed on Slasher's beak.

Pam glanced down at the poop deck. 'Keep scrubbing!' she yelled. 'Or

I'll make you do the Captain's poo bucket. He had curried eel for dinner last night.' She flew off.

Jimmy fluttered down towards the poop deck and perched on the railing. He looked at Thug and Slasher with distaste. 'Clean yourselves up, you two.' He grimaced. 'You're a disgrace to magpies.'

'Sorry, Boss.' The magpies hopped into the bucket and splashed about. They hopped out, dripping with filthy water.

'What did she say?' Thug asked eagerly.

'Yeah, what's the secret?' Slasher echoed.

Jimmy glanced round. 'It seems like we've landed on our feet after all.' Jimmy told the gang about the mermaid in the casket. He told them about the message in the bottle. He told them about Fishhook Frank being marooned on a desert island and how Fishhook would lead them to the casket when the Captain had captured him. He told them about how to summon the mermaid with the rhyme.

'A mermaid!' Thug sat down on the mop. 'That's lovely, that is. It's like a fairytale! 'Ere, Jimmy, do you think she'll give us some of her hair to make a nest snuggler with?'

'She'll give us anything we want, Thug,' Jimmy said patiently. 'That's the point.'

'Anything?' Thug repeated. His beady eyes grew round. 'You mean like shiny things.'

'Yeah,' Jimmy grinned. 'Shiny things, worms, a new nest under the pier, clean washing to poo on, revenge on Atticus Claw. You name it: the mermaid will give it to us. Once the Captain finds the casket all we have to do is say the rhyme.'

'Magic mermaid on the shore, please grant me what I'm wishing for,' the words rolled out of Slasher's beak. 'Chaka-chaka-chaka-chaka-chaka!'

'That's nice, that is, Slash,' Thug said. 'Very poetic.'

'Thanks, Thug,' Slasher said modestly. 'I made up the last bit.' Suddenly a thought struck him. 'What if the mermaid can't understand us, though?' he said anxiously. 'What if she can't speak Magpie?'

'Of course she can speak Magpie,' Thug said promptly. 'She's magic.'

'But what if Captain Black Beard-Jumper says the rhyme first?' Slasher said doubtfully. 'The mermaid will grant his wishes instead of ours.'

'Relax, Slasher,' Jimmy Magpie soothed. 'He won't. Think about it. Thug's right. The mermaid understands Magpie,' he said slyly, 'but the Captain doesn't.'

'I still don't get it, Boss,' Slasher said.

'That's cos you're stupid!' Jimmy flared. 'You've got to use your brain. The Captain won't think twice if he hears a bunch of magpies chattering, will he? He won't know we're summoning the mermaid in Magpie. By the time he realises what's going on, it'll be too late.' Jimmy's eyes shone bright with glee. 'The mermaid will be ours. Until then all *you* have to do is keep scrubbing.' Jimmy made himself comfortable on a pile of nets. 'And all I have to do is lie back and wait.'

Two days later . . .

At a busy port in the Moluccan islands of Indonesia, Commander Whale was introducing Mr Tucker and his crew to their new vessel.

Atticus crept along the pontoon after the children. The temperature was roasting . All the humans were wearing loose cotton clothes and hats. Atticus's paws felt hot and sticky. His fur was dusty. He wanted a drink of water. He couldn't wait to get out of the sun and into the shade.

'She's small enough to navigate the islands,' the Commander explained. 'But big enough to withstand heavy weather.'

It took Atticus a moment to work out he was talking about their ship.

'Here we are!'

The yacht was about fifteen metres long. It was made of wood. A tall mast extended into the sky. It had a rope ladder attached to the top of it, which stretched all the way down to the railing that ran around the edge. Taut metal ropes criss-crossed like spider webs from the mast to different points on the vessel. Beneath them, lengths of rope lay in neat coils on the deck. It all looked horribly complicated to Atticus. He'd never been on a yacht before. He'd once been on Mr Tucker's fishing boat, but that didn't have sails. Apart from that he'd only ever been on a cruise ship, which was like a floating hotel. You didn't even know you were moving.

'I like her name,' Mr Tucker said. '*Destiny*.' He rolled the word around on his tongue.

Destiny. It was one of those words that said a lot in not very many letters, Atticus thought dismally. He wondered what their destiny would be: whether they would save Inspector Cheddar in time, or not.

'There are three cabins,' the Commander explained. He led the way down the narrow steps into the hold. Atticus padded after him. He

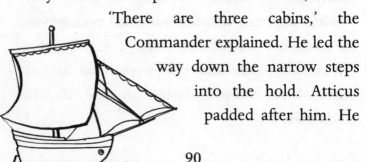

90

thought he might melt. It was even hotter below deck. A seating area led on to a small kitchen. Beyond that a door led to the cabins.

'The boat has all the latest computer navigation equipment,' the Commander pointed to a screen. 'And there's a radio so you can keep in touch with me on the frigate. We've asked the Americans to send over a smaller ship for us so we can provide back-up in an emergency, but it might take a few days. Until then you're on your own.'

A porter clambered down the steps with their bags and put them in the cabins.

'I think that's it,' the Commander said. He shook hands with Mr Tucker. 'Good luck.'

The Commander and the porter disappeared.

'I'll go and unpack the first aid kit,' Mrs Cheddar said. 'Are you sure you're okay, darling?' she asked her husband anxiously. 'You don't want a lie down or anything?'

'No,' Inspector Cheddar sounded melancholy. He took his notebook out of his pocket. 'Besides, I'm still on police duty.' He scowled at Atticus. 'Which I take more seriously than *some* officers I could mention.'

Atticus tried to ignore him. He wished Inspector Cheddar wouldn't keep harping on about things. It wasn't exactly helping.

'Put these on.' Mr Tucker gave each crew member a life jacket. There was even one for Atticus. Michael held him while Callie put his front paws through the holes and clipped up the straps. It made Atticus even hotter. He thought he might faint.

'Ready?' Mr Tucker said. 'Then let's get under way.'

They followed Mr Tucker back up the steps to the cockpit. He started the engine. Mrs Tucker untied the ropes that held the boat to its mooring. It slipped away from the pontoon and out to sea.

As the noise and bustle of the port faded, Atticus began to feel a bit brighter. The sea was calm. A cool breeze played about his whiskers. He found a shady spot on the deck and lay down for a snooze. Maybe sailing wasn't so bad after all.

'Atticus!' Mr Tucker roared. 'What do youze thinks you're doing? Go fooorrre and check the spinnaker.'

Atticus looked at him blankly. *What was he talking about?*

92

'Hurry up!'

Atticus got up with a sigh and headed towards the rear of the boat.

'I said foooorrre, not aft!' Mr Tucker yelled. 'Don't youze knows your bow from your stern?!!'

Atticus didn't.

'Don't worry, Atticus,' Mrs Tucker whispered. 'You'll get the hang of it. The bow is the front of the boat. The stern is the back.'

Atticus frowned. *Why couldn't they just call it front and back if that was what it was?*

'I'll do it, Herman.' Mrs Tucker picked her way carefully to the front of the boat.

'Kids: hoist the mainsail!' Mr Tucker shouted. 'Use the winch.'

Callie and Michael pulled on a rope. A huge white sail rose up the mast. Callie wrapped the end of the rope around a cylindrical drum. Then she placed a handle in the centre of the drum and turned it.

That must be the winch, Atticus thought. He watched, fascinated, as the sail tightened.

'Set the jib!'

Inspector and Mrs Cheddar took hold of two

more ropes. A second sail unfurled outwards towards the front of the boat from the mast.

Mr Tucker cut the engine. Gradually he turned the wheel until the sails filled with wind.

Atticus felt the yacht spring forward. It cut through the water. The wind whipped at his whiskers. They were moving really fast! He had no idea a wind-powered boat could shift so quickly! He wished Mimi were there to keep him company. She would love this.

'I'm starving!' Michael said.

'Me too!' Callie agreed. 'Sailing always makes me hungry.'

'Come on, then,' Mrs Cheddar said. 'I'll get you something to eat.'

'Atticus, take the wheel,' Mr Tucker ordered. 'I'm going to help Mrs Tucker with the spinnaker. Make sure you hold our course.' He limped off along the deck.

Atticus was left in the cockpit. What was the spinnaker? And what did Mr Tucker mean 'hold our course'? Was it something to do with steering the boat? He turned the wheel cautiously with his paw. The sails started to flutter.

CRACK!

Suddenly the boat listed violently to one side.

Atticus slid along the cockpit. He hid his face in his paws. They must have hit something!

'Atticus!' Mr Tucker was beside him. 'In the name of Poseidon, what the hake do youze think you're doing?' He took hold of the wheel. Gradually the boat steadied.

Atticus peeped through his paws. The sails had somehow moved across the boat to the other side when he wasn't looking!

'I told youze to hold our course, not sail by the lee!' Mr Tucker complained. 'I wish Bones was here,' he muttered. 'That cat was a brilliant sailor.'

Atticus felt deflated. He had a feeling he'd be hearing a lot more about Bones over the next few days.

Mrs Tucker joined them in the cockpit. 'Atticus doesn't understand sailing, Herman,' Mrs Tucker told her husband. 'He's never been on a yacht before. You need to explain things to him.'

'I's don't have time for that!' Mr Tucker said grumpily. 'And anyways, I never had to explain it to

Bones!'

'All right, then I will,' Mrs Tucker said. 'It's like this, Atticus,' she pointed to a horizontal beam of wood that stuck out from the mast beneath the mainsail. 'That's the boom. When you sail away from the wind, the sail fills with air. That's what makes us go forward. But if you turn the wheel too much, the wind gets the other side of the sail and the boom swings across and makes the boat unsteady. It's called an accidental gybe.'

'It's boomin' dangerous,' Mr Tucker glowered. 'We could have broached!'

'He means the boat could have been blown flat,' Mrs Tucker explained. 'What you *should* do is bring the boom across gradually so that everyone is prepared for it.'

Atticus listened glumly. He didn't think he'd ever get the hang of it . . . unlike the amazing Bones.

Callie and Michael reappeared with Mrs Cheddar.

'Where's Dad?' Callie asked.

Atticus looked along the deck. There was no sign of Inspector Cheddar. The boom took up the space where he had been standing a few minutes earlier. He felt proud of himself for remembering what it was called.

'For cod's sake!' Mr Tucker exploded. 'Atticus has knocked him off the boat!'

Atticus was horrified. He hadn't meant to knock Inspector Cheddar off the boat! He hoped nobody thought he'd done it on purpose!

'Quick, Edna,' Mr Tucker ordered, 'turn her around! MAN OVERBOARD!! All hands on deck!'

Mrs Tucker took the wheel.

'There aren't any sharks here, are there?' Michael sounded petrified.

Nobody answered. Atticus saw Mr and Mrs Tucker exchange worried looks.

'Don't youze worry, kids,' Mr Tucker said. 'We'll find your dad. Come and give Mrs Tucker a hand, while your mum steers.' The two women swapped places. Mrs Cheddar took the helm. Her face was white.

Mrs Tucker and the children went to the other end of the deck and started to pull down the big sail at the front.

Mr Tucker did the same with the other two sails.

Atticus milled around the cockpit. He felt helpless. No one had given him a job. Everyone seemed to have forgotten he was even there.

Mrs Cheddar started the engine. She turned the boat so they were facing in the direction they had just come from. The yacht motored towards the spot where the accident had happened.

Atticus scanned the sea.

'There he is!' Michael shouted. 'Port side!'

Inspector Cheddar was bobbing up and down in the water some distance away on the left of the boat. He waved. 'Help!' he shouted faintly. 'Help!'

'Cut the engine!' Mr Tucker ordered. 'Or we'll chop his legs off with the propeller.'

Mrs Cheddar did as she was told. There was an eerie silence as the boat drifted towards the Inspector.

Atticus suddenly felt very small and frightened. There were no other boats to be seen. They were out of sight of land. It was as if they were the only sailors on the whole big ocean. If they couldn't rescue Inspector Cheddar, there was no one else who could help them.

'Throw him a line,' Mr Tucker shouted.

Mrs Tucker picked up a coil of rope.

'Wait, what's that?' Michael pointed. 'Over there.'

Atticus's green eyes swept the horizon. A thin grey triangle stuck up through the waves. It was making its way swiftly towards Inspector Cheddar.

'Shaarrrkk!' Mr Tucker yelled. 'Give me the rope, Edna. We'll only get one throw.'

Mrs Tucker handed him the coil of rope.

Mr Tucker made a lasso with one end and leaned over the rail.

'Quick!' yelled Michael.

The shark was closing in fast.

SHWIPP!

Mr Tucker threw the lasso. It looped through the air and landed with a splash beside Inspector Cheddar.

Inspector Cheddar grabbed it. He wriggled it over his head and under his arms.

'Hold on!' Mr Tucker attached his end of the

rope to the drum. 'Give me the winch handle!'

Michael thrust it towards him.

CRANK! CRANK! CRANK! CRANK!

Mr Tucker's thick arms whirled the handle round and round.

Inspector Cheddar flew through the water: the lasso around his armpits, his hands grasping the rope. The shark was close behind.

All Atticus could do was watch. *Come on, Mr Tucker*, he thought. *Come on! Please don't let him be eaten!*

'He's not going to make it!' Callie screamed.

The shark was gaining.

'It thinks your dad's a seal!' Mr Tucker cried. 'Shaarks love seals, they do. It's their favourite food.'

Suddenly Atticus had an idea. *His* favourite food was sardines. Maybe sharks liked them too! He raced down the steps into the galley and pulled open the fridge with his paws. It was jammed with food. At the back was a bag of fresh sardines. He pulled the bag out and struggled back up the steps, dragging it in his mouth. He dropped it beside Mrs Tucker.

Mrs Tucker picked the bag up. 'Good thinking, Atticus!' She ripped it open.

Inspector Cheddar had reached the ship. He gripped the ladder and started to climb. The shark was only metres away.

'Hurry, Dad!' Callie screeched.

The shark leapt out of the water, its mouth open.

Atticus caught a glimpse of rows of razor-sharp teeth.

Mrs Tucker threw the sardines out to sea: away from the side of the boat.

The shark caught the powerful scent of the fish. It arched backwards to catch them.

SNAP!

It gobbled them up and fell back into the water.

Mr Tucker leaned over the rail and hauled Inspector Cheddar on to the deck.

Inspector Cheddar collapsed. The children and Mrs Cheddar raced over to him.

Atticus wanted to go too, but something told him he might not be welcome. He hung back.

He felt a hand on his head. It was Mrs Tucker. 'You saved his life, Atticus,' she said, scratching the spot between his ears. 'Don't forget that.'

Atticus tried to purr but he couldn't. He might have saved Inspector Cheddar's life in the end, but the fact remained it was him who had knocked Inspector Cheddar overboard in the first place! He remembered what Mimi said about learning from your mistakes. He didn't think he *could* on this occasion, even though he wanted to. However hard he tried, Atticus decided, he would always be useless as a ship's cat.

It wasn't until late the following afternoon that they arrived at the island where Mr Tucker believed Fishhook Frank was marooned.

Atticus glanced at the sky. The sun was beginning to set. He counted up the days on his claws. It was Sunday. There were only five more days until Friday the thirteenth – when the curse of the black spot would strike Inspector Cheddar at sunset. Fishhook Frank had to be here. He just had to. They were running out of time.

They anchored in a cove some distance away from the beach. 'We caarrn't go any closer,' Mr Tucker explained. 'In case we run aground.'

'Are you sure this is the place, Herman?' Mrs Tucker scanned the beach with her binoculars. Behind the beach was a dark jungle. 'There's no sign of anyone.'

'Fishhook's probably hiding somewhere,' Mr Tucker said, 'to make sure we's friendly.'

'Unless Black Beard-Jumper got here first,' Mrs Tucker reminded him.

There was an uncomfortable silence. If that was the case, Atticus thought gloomily, they were sunk.

'Black Beard-Jumper's never been here before,' Mr Tucker said confidently. 'It'll be haarrd for him to find this place from Fishhook's message. So I reckons there's a good chance we beat him to it. Now come on. We'll take the rib.' He led the way to the stern.

The rib, Atticus discovered, wasn't (as he first hoped) a juicy bone with meat on it, but another one of Mr Tucker's nautical nightmares. It was a rubber dinghy with an outboard motor, which had thus far been sneakily attached to the ship in such a way that Atticus hadn't seen it. Mr Tucker lowered it carefully on to the water with the aid of yet more rope and some pulleys. The Tuckers and the children climbed in using the ladder. Atticus tried to do the same, but found he couldn't climb backwards on the rope treads. And he was too scared to jump. There was then a tricky moment while Mrs Cheddar, who was staying on board with the Inspector, lifted Atticus carefully over the side in a canvas bag and handed him to Mrs Tucker, while the dinghy pitched and rolled.

Mr Tucker watched disapprovingly 'Bones would have been down that ladder like a monkey,' he commented.

Although he'd never met Bones, Atticus was beginning to seriously dislike her. She sounded like an awful show-off.

Once Mrs Tucker had removed Atticus from the canvas bag, Mr Tucker let out the throttle and the dinghy shot off. The five rescuers bumped through the sea towards the shore, the dinghy chopping through the waves. Spray flew in all directions – mainly, it seemed to Atticus, in his! The water drenched his whiskers and clogged his ears. It trickled off his nose and made his handkerchief damp. Then, when he tried to shelter in the bottom of the dinghy, he sat in a cold puddle. His tail was soaked. Atticus clawed his way back on to the bench next to Mrs Tucker and tried to lick it clean. PTTTHHH!

he spat. The water tasted disgusting.

'It's salt water, Atticus,' Mrs Tucker explained. 'The sea has salt in it. You can't drink it or you'll be sick.' She picked him up and wrapped him in a fluffy towel which she'd brought in case the children felt cold. His head poked out from the parcel.

Callie giggled. 'Atticus looks like a baby,' she said.

Atticus felt cross. It was nice to see Callie laughing for a change but not when she was laughing at him! He wasn't a baby. He was still a police cat sergeant. Or at least he was for the time being anyway. He wriggled free.

The dinghy approached the beach. Mr Tucker switched off the engine. He jumped out with Michael and the two of them hauled the boat through the shallows and up on to the sand. The others clambered after them. Mrs Tucker put Atticus down. He could feel the sand sticking to his damp fur and clogging his paws. He glanced at the sky. The crimson rim of the sun was still visible on the horizon, but it was setting rapidly. In another half an hour it would be dark.

'It's definitely the right place.' Mr Tucker looked around. 'This is where me and Frank camped before we set off on our voyage to find the caarrsket.'

'Look!' Michael pointed at a pile of driftwood. 'Someone's been collecting logs.'

'That'll be Fishhook,' Mr Tucker said confidently.

'Over here!' Callie shouted. 'Someone's had a fire going.' The sand was dark where it mingled with ash. A couple of charred logs lay half buried.

'That'll be Fishhook too,' Mr Tucker said. 'To attract passing ships. 'E's definitely 'ere somewhere.'

'I don't want to burst your bubble, Herman, but the fire's been kicked out.' Mrs Tucker bent down and examined the remains. 'And there are footprints all over the place. Someone else has been here, besides Fishhook.'

Atticus padded over to take a look. Some of the footprints were huge. They had a round toe and a square heel, as if they had been made by an enormous pair of boots. Atticus shivered. He glanced at Mrs Tucker.

'Captain Black Beard-Jumper's,' she confirmed.

Callie's eyes filled with tears. 'That means Black Beard-Jumper's got Fishhook Frank,' she sniffed. 'Now we'll never find the mermaid.'

Atticus knew what that meant. He nudged Callie's hand to comfort her.

She stroked him absently.

'Never's a big word, Callie Cheddar,' Mrs Tucker said firmly. 'Maybe Fishhook left a clue.'

'He might have made a map!' Michael suggested eagerly. 'And hidden it from Captain Black Beard-Jumper in case one of his friends came to rescue him later.'

'Come to think of it, there was a map!' Mr Tucker gasped. 'Fishhook staarrted it when we was on our voyage together to find the mermaid all them years ago. 'E never got to finish it that time cos I got me leg clipped off.'

'But he would have finished it when he went back!' Callie wasn't crying any more. Her eyes were bright.

A map! Atticus felt his fur prickle with excitement. He began to purr.

'Is there anywhere you can think of he'd hide something like that, Herman?' Mrs Tucker asked her husband.

'Aye.' Mr Tucker nodded slowly. 'There is. Follow me, everyone.' He started towards the jungle.

'It's getting awfully dark, Herman,' Mrs Tucker said doubtfully. 'Do you think we should wait until the morning? Goodness knows what's lurking in that forest.'

Mr Tucker shook his head. 'We's already behind Black Beard-Jumper. We's can't wait. We's got to find that map.' He glanced at the children. 'Kids, you follow behind me. Then you, Edna. Atticus, you take the rear. Watch out for snakes.' He hobbled up the beach, dragging his wooden leg through the sand.

Snakes! Atticus hated snakes. He wondered what he was supposed to do if he saw one. He scrambled along the sand behind Mrs Tucker.

The party entered the jungle.

It was even darker under the trees and much cooler. Atticus glanced up. The trees weren't the sort you got in Littleton-on-Sea or even Monte Carlo. They were taller with great thick trunks and leaves as big as lily pads that shut out the sky. Strange brightly coloured flowers blossomed around their bases. Vines twisted round the trunks and hung in thick ropes from the branches.

The procession threaded its way through the gloomy jungle. The trees were full of the shrieks and cackles of animals. The mournful cry of unseen birds echoed from high up in the canopy of dense leaves.

Atticus felt his hackles rise. He had the uncomfortable feeling they were being watched.

His sharp ears caught a whisper of movement behind him. He turned round quickly, just in time to catch a glimpse of a dark shadow slipping away into the undergrowth. He couldn't tell what it was. An animal of some sort, definitely. But whether it was a snake, or a mongoose, or even a panther, he couldn't say. He waited for a moment but the animal didn't reappear.

Reluctantly he padded on after the others.

After a little while they came to a clearing.

'It's still here,' Mr Tucker said in a satisfied voice. 'I's thought so.'

In the middle of the clearing Atticus was amazed to see a small log cabin. Flowers grew out of the turf roof and the walls were decorated with bright candy-coloured shells. It looked welcoming in the gathering dusk.

'That's so cool!' Michael cried.

'It's like the witch's cottage in *Hansel and Gretel*!' Even Callie was smiling at the sight of the little wooden house. 'Except it's covered in shells, not sweets!'

'That's exactly how Fishhook described it!' Mr Tucker exclaimed. 'Like the cottage in *Hansel and Gretel*. He loved stories, did Fishhook.'

Atticus thought he might like Fishhook Frank. He loved stories too.

'Me and Fishhook, we's made it before we set out to look for the mermaid together,' Mr Tucker said proudly. 'Nice and snug it is. Come and look inside.'

'Maybe Fishhook left the map here!' Callie exclaimed excitedly. 'Let's go and see.' She raced up to the door and opened it. Her face fell.

Atticus wondered what was the matter. He chased after her and looked in. His heart sank.

The little cabin had been ransacked.

The pirates had beaten them to it.

1·2

Inside the cabin smashed plates lay in jagged pieces. The straw mattresses had been torn into clumps and the coarse linen sheets shredded into ribbons. Wooden boxes full of supplies spilled what remained of their contents on to the floor. A thin covering of feathers lay like a dusting of snow over the chaos: two pillows had been slashed with a knife and emptied over the rest.

There was no sign of a map.

'It looks like someone got here before we did,' Mrs Tucker said grimly. 'Black Beard-Jumper and his men, I'm guessing. What do you say, Herman?'

Mr Tucker nodded dismally.

'They've taken it!' Callie said despondently. 'I was right, we'll never find the mermaid.'

This time Mrs Tucker didn't correct her.

Michael looked downcast.

Atticus thought fast. Just because Black Beard-Jumper's men had turned the place over didn't mean they had found what they were looking for. Atticus forgot about the gathering darkness and the jungle that lay between them and the relative safety of the ship and tried to think like a detective.

Inspector Cheddar had once told him the best way to find clues at a crime scene was to imagine that you were the criminal. (That had been a lot easier for Atticus than for Inspector Cheddar because Atticus had actually once *been* a criminal.) Maybe, considered Atticus, it was the same for pirates. *If I were Fishhook Frank* he thought *and I was trying to hide something, what would I do?*

He frowned. Something that Callie had said a minute ago nagged at him. He tried to remember. *The witch's cottage from Hansel and Gretel.* That was it! And according to Mr Tucker, Fishhook Frank had called it that too.

Atticus had seen the story in Callie's big storybook. The first time Hansel and Gretel were abandoned in the woods they left a trail of stones in the wood for their father to find them. The second time they left a trail of breadcrumbs, which the birds ate. Fishhook Frank liked stories. Maybe he'd had the same idea. Maybe he'd left a trail leading to the map.

Atticus went back outside and scanned the clearing. He wasn't sure exactly what he was looking for: some kind of path made out of . . . *Wait! There!* A small metallic object gleamed in the gloom. Beyond it another lay another! And another! Fishhooks! Atticus purred with pleasure. Of course! It was brilliant. Fishhook Frank had laid a trail of fishhooks for his friends to follow just in case he was rescued by the wrong pirates!

Atticus padded from one fishhook to the next. The trail wasn't straight. Sometimes he had to look hard in the dirt or under a plant to find the next hook. But gradually, paw by paw, Atticus found himself being led to the edge of the jungle behind the cottage.

The trail stopped abruptly at a gnarled tree

stump. The final fishhook lay beside it in the grass. The map must be hidden in the hollow stump. Atticus surveyed the tree stump with distaste. It was nearly dark now, but it was still light enough to make out that the stump's nooks and crannies were crawling with beetles. He closed his eyes, stretched out a paw and felt into the tree trunk. His stomach squirmed. He could feel the creepy-crawlies scratching at the fur on his foreleg. He gritted his teeth and dug deeper into the mouldy interior. His paw touched something hard and slippery. He tried to catch hold of it but the object slipped out of his grasp. Atticus took a deep breath. He wriggled closer to the tree trunk, trying to ignore the flutter and hum of the beetles on his whiskers. He extended his paw further into the trunk. There! Growling with the effort he managed to hook his paw around the object and flick it closer. Sitting on his haunches he put both paws into the hollow, took hold of the object's curved sides and pulled it out.

Atticus brushed the beetles off his whiskers and gave his paw a quick wash with his tongue. PHHTT! The leaf mould tasted even worse than seawater.

He sat back and examined his find. It was an old biscuit tin. He started to ease the lid off with his claws.

Just then he heard a familiar whisper of movement in the trees. Atticus looked up, startled. This time he glimpsed more than a shadow. This time he saw the animal that had been following them earlier.

A small black cat with a grizzled muzzle and a crooked tail stepped out of the darkness and eyed him warily.

Atticus placed the biscuit tin down carefully. The strange cat took a step towards it. Its eyes shifted towards the tin then back to Atticus. It took another step then reached out a paw and tried to hook the tin by the lid with its claws. Atticus pushed the tin out of the way and stood in front of it. He didn't know what to do. The cat was a female, but it looked intent on a fight. Atticus hated fighting. And he certainly didn't want to do it with an old lady cat.

'Atticus!' A voice shouted. It was Michael. 'Where are you?'

At the sound of a human voice, the black cat hesitated.

'There he is!' Callie yelled.

The beam of a powerful torch wobbled across the tree stump and fell on Atticus.

The black cat started to back away.

'Wait!' Michael said. 'What's that?'

The roving light caught the small black cat in the eye. She blinked, momentarily dazzled.

The humans rushed over, all except Mr Tucker, who limped. When he saw the small black cat, to Atticus's amazement he gave a yelp of joy.

'Bones!' he cried. 'It's you! After all these years! What a stroke of luck!'

13

Back at the ship, Bones bounced out of the dinghy and zipped up the ladder after the children. It was pitch black now but the ship had powerful lights which guided the dinghy back through the bumpy surf.

'See?' Mr Tucker beamed. 'What did I tell youze? That cat's got claass.'

Atticus regarded Bones sourly as she leapt athletically on to the deck. They hadn't exchanged any meows yet, only suspicious looks. *What was Bones doing on the island anyway?* Atticus wondered. *Had Fishhook Frank left her there? And why did she hide from Mr Tucker?* Atticus was sure it was Bones that had been following them through the jungle. She must have seen Mr Tucker. *So why didn't she*

119

want him to know she was there? And what did she want with the biscuit tin? Did she know it contained Fishhook Frank's map?

Atticus felt instinctively that something about Bones didn't quite add up.

'Come on, Atticus!' Mr Tucker shouted.

Atticus placed a foot on the first rung of the ladder and began to haul himself up, paw by paw. He wasn't going let Bones see him being hoisted on board in a canvas bag!

Inspector and Mrs Cheddar greeted everybody on deck.

'We were so worried about you when we saw you head off into the jungle!' Mrs Cheddar hugged the children. She looked past Atticus to see if anyone else was coming up the ladder. 'Where's Fishhook Frank?' she asked.

'Gone,' Mr Tucker said. 'Captain Black Beard-Jumper got to him first.'

Inspector Cheddar's expression was stricken. 'I'm doomed,' he cried. 'Doomed to die a horrible cruel death!'

'Don't worry, Dad! Michael said hastily. 'The good news is Atticus found Bones.'

'I's never thought I would see her again!' Mr Tucker said ecstatically. 'Me old friend, Bones!'

'And Bones found this.' Michael held out the biscuit tin.

WHAT? Atticus couldn't believe his ears. Michael had got everything round the wrong way. It was he who had found the biscuit tin. And Bones who had found him! He glanced at Bones. But Bones was busy tying a complicated knot in a piece of rope with her teeth. She didn't look up.

'I don't want a biscuit,' Inspector Cheddar complained. 'I just had dinner.'

'No, Dad! You don't get it! There's a map inside which shows where the casket's hidden,' Callie said. 'Fishook Frank made it.'

Inspector Cheddar clasped his hands together in joy. 'Well done, Bones!' he said. 'You would make an excellent police cat detective.' He glared at Atticus. 'Unlike some cats I could mention.'

This time Atticus glared back at him. He'd had enough of Inspector Cheddar and his rude comments. He'd found the biscuit tin and that was that. Maybe one day Inspector Cheddar would thank him for it, if he ever discovered the truth.

Mr Tucker rattled the biscuit tin. 'Now let's get below and see what Fishhook's got for us.'

Atticus looked around for Bones, but she had disappeared. He padded after the others into the cabin. To his surprise, Bones was already down there, sweeping the floor with a duster tied to her tail.

'That's it, Bones,' Mr Tucker said. 'Trust you to keep everything shipshape!' He gave Bones a quick pat on the head. 'Good to have you back as me ship's cat after all these years.'

Atticus didn't really mind Bones replacing him. He'd never wanted to be ship's cat in the first place. But there was still something odd about the way Bones was behaving. First she completely ignored Mr Tucker on the island: now she couldn't do enough for him. And the biscuit tin. *Why had she tried to take it?* Atticus still couldn't work it out. It didn't make sense. Unless . . .

Mr Tucker removed the lid from the biscuit tin and took out a large piece of rolled parchment. He spread the parchment on the table.

Atticus jumped on to the table beside Bones, who had somehow managed to get there first. Her eyes were glued to the map.

The map was the size of a poster. A strip had been torn from one corner: the strip that Fishhook Frank had used to write the message in the bottle, Atticus guessed. It was the same thick yellow paper.

Atticus found his eyes were glued to the map too. It was covered in extraordinary pictures drawn in different coloured inks. It showed mountainous waves and swirling whirlpools and jagged flashes of lightning. It showed a sea swarming with creatures that Atticus had never seen before and a ship battling for survival amidst the writhing tentacles of a giant squid. It showed fire spouting from a conical mountain and a path that led into the mountain under a waterfall of lava.

Atticus's eyes travelled downwards. Deep beneath the mountain lay an underground lagoon.

And in the centre of the lagoon, across a path of stepping stones, was an X.

'That's where it be,' Mr Tucker said. 'X marks the spot where the caarrsket lies.' He placed a thumb on the bottom right-hand corner of the map.

'Where are we at the moment, Herman?' Mrs Tucker asked.

Mr Tucker placed his other thumb on the top left-hand corner furthest away from the X. 'Here,' he said. 'We's got to cross all this to reach it.'

'Mr Tucker, when you went in search of the casket before with Fishhook Frank, how far did you get?' Michael asked.

Mr Tucker scratched his beard-jumper. 'We's sailed through the Sea of Calamity and past the Whirlpool of Doom,' he remembered. 'We's survived the Storm of Stupefaction. It was when we got partway through the Ocean of Terror that disaster struck.' His hand went to his wooden leg. 'That's where the magical sea creatures be,' he explained. 'Including the man-eating plankton.'

Man-eating plankton?! Atticus hoped they didn't eat cats as well – only men.

'Is that what the little green things with big teeth are?' Callie asked, pointing at the swarm of strange sea creatures.

'Aye. They nip worse than piranhas, they do,'

Mr Tucker said. 'Strip the flesh off your bones in seconds.'

Atticus swallowed.

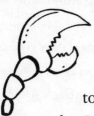

'But they's nothing compared to the other creatures what lurk in the Ocean of Terror,' Mr Tucker went on. 'Take the giant lobster. Bigger than a whale, it is, with a claw the size of a sailor.' His face was grim. 'It was that beast what clipped off me leg.'

There was a moment's silence in the cabin in memory of Mr Tucker's leg.

'How did you . . . you know . . . survive when it happened?' Michael asked.

Atticus flattened his ears. He was squeamish about blood. He wasn't sure he wanted to know.

'Fishhook made a tourniquet out of rope,' Mr Tucker explained, 'and tied it round what was left of me leg to stop the blood gushing out. I used part of me beard-jumper as a dressing. Then Bones patched it up with a bit of sail cloth. Most loyal ship's cat ever, Bones!'

Atticus looked hard at Bones. Captain Black Beard-Jumper had said much the same thing about

126

her just before he cursed Inspector Cheddar at the beard-jumper competition.

Mr Tucker clapped his hands. 'We'd best make a staarrt tonight if we's to catch the *Doubloon*. I'll take the first watch.' He got up from the table.

'We should tell the Commander what's happened,' Mrs Cheddar said.

Mrs Tucker sat down at the radio and placed the headphones over her ears. She twiddled a few knobs and spoke into the mouthpiece. '*Destiny* calling *Clover*,' she said. 'Do you copy?' *Clover* was the name of the Commander's ship.

'Mum, can I borrow your phone to take a picture of the map?' Michael asked. 'We can scan it into the computer and send it to the Commander. There's no signal out here.'

Mrs Cheddar rummaged in her bag. 'Here you are. I think there's a tiny bit of battery left.'

Michael snapped a few close-ups of the map. 'Thanks.' He fed a lead from the computer into the phone and tapped a few keys. Nothing happened. The screen was blank. 'That's funny,' he said. 'I can't get the computer to work.'

'And I can't get the radio to work either,' Mrs

127

Tucker said. '*Destiny* calling *Clover*,' she repeated. 'Do you copy?' The only sound that came from the headphones was a loud hissing. Atticus could hear it from where he sat on the table. 'Herman, check the power.'

Mr Tucker opened a cupboard beneath the computer. Inside was a gauge like a clock, with numbers ticking round on a display. 'It's on,' he said.

Atticus jumped down to take a look.

'I think I've found the problem!' Michael was checking the cables. He pulled a fistful of loose wires from the back of the computer station. 'Look!' The ends were frayed as if something had chewed through them.

'Rats!' Mr Tucker spat. 'I's bet they got on board when the ship was in poorrt. Soon as they saw Atticus they must have disappeared smaartish.'

Atticus frowned. He hadn't seen any rats. And there was no evidence that they'd ever been on board. Rats left droppings. They left fur balls and fleas, not to mention a nasty smell of rat wee. The ship was as clean as a whistle and had been from the moment they'd stepped on deck. Whatever it was that had chewed the wires it wasn't rats. And if it wasn't rats, Atticus thought, it could only be one thing.

'So, we can't reach the Commander,' Mrs Cheddar said slowly.

'No,' Mrs Tucker said. 'It looks like we're on our own.'

'Don't youze worry: I knows what I's doing,' Mr Tucker said briskly. 'Bones, you can take over the wheel when youze finished dusting the floor. Atticus, stay with Bones and don't touch anything.'

Everyone disappeared on deck. Only Atticus and Bones were left in the cabin.

'Do you want some help?' Atticus offered. He didn't really want to help. He wanted some answers. But it broke the ice.

'No,' Bones said shortly. 'You heard Mr Tucker.'

Atticus said nothing further. He waited.

The silence in the cabin was broken by the swish of Bones's tail. After a few minutes Bones untied the duster, folded it neatly and started towards the steps, avoiding Atticus's eye.

'Oh no you don't.' Atticus stood in her way.

Bones still didn't look directly at him. 'Didn't

you hear the Captain?' she muttered. 'He wants me on deck.'

'And you always do what the Captain says,' Atticus said softly. 'Don't you, Bones? Most loyal ship's cat, aren't you? Just like Mr Tucker said.'

Bones said nothing.

'Only it's not Captain Tucker you're loyal to, is it, Bones?' Atticus whispered. 'It's Captain Black Beard-Jumper.'

'No!' Bones let out a choked meow. 'You've got it all wrong.'

'Have I?' Atticus said. 'Then tell me why you chewed those cables.'

Bones was silent for a moment.

'Well?' Atticus said. 'What have you got to say for yourself?'

Bones took a deep breath. 'My mother was Captain Black Beard-Jumper's first ship's cat,' she began.

Atticus was startled. He hadn't expected that. *What did Bones's mother have to do with it?* Whatever it was he didn't think anything Bones had to say could make up for her betrayal.

'Go on,' he said coldly.

'She was beautiful,' Bones continued. 'A silky black animal with the longest whiskers anyone had ever seen and the deepest green eyes. I don't know where she came from originally. Somewhere in

India I think. The story on board the *Golden Doubloon* was that the Captain bought her from a mystic and that there was something magical about her too.' Bones sighed. 'Whatever the real story was, the Captain believed she brought him luck.' She paused.

Atticus said nothing. He still couldn't fathom where Bones was going with this.

'She sailed everywhere with him. She sailed the China Seas and the Pacific. She sailed the Indian Ocean and around the Caribbean. Then one day, when they were in port in Africa, she met my father. She told me he was handsome,' Bones purred softly. 'A tabby, like you.'

Atticus couldn't help purring back. It seemed like a long time since anyone had paid him a compliment. And he *was* handsome. He was pleased Bones had noticed. Then he frowned. He wasn't going to let Bones flatter her way out of this. 'So what?' he asked. 'What has any of this to do with you chewing the cables?'

'I'm getting to that,' Bones said.

Atticus could hear the sadness in her voice. He decided not to interrupt again.

'My mother wanted to stay with my father. They hid in the port but Captain Black Beard-Jumper sent the crew out looking for her. He didn't want to lose his lucky charm.' Bones's voice faltered. 'They found them. They killed my father and dragged my mother back to the ship.'

Atticus remained silent. It sounded like she'd never spoken to any other cat before about what happened.

'A few weeks later,' Bones said, 'she had five kittens. I was the firstborn. And I was the only black one. The others were tabby after my father: like you.' She took a deep breath.

Atticus wondered what was coming next.

'Captain Black Beard-Jumper had no use for them. He said they were common. He said he didn't want them. He said only a pure-bred cat was good enough to be ship's cat on the *Golden Doubloon*.' A tear trickled on to Bones's whiskers. 'Do you know what he did?'

Atticus shook his head. He put out a paw and wiped the tear away. He'd never seen a cat cry before. Poor Bones! Whatever it was, it must be something dreadful.

'When they were two days old,' Bones carried on with an effort, 'he put them in a sack with a stone and tied it up with rope. Then he threw them into the sea. He was laughing when he did it.'

Atticus was horrified. He couldn't believe anyone could be so cruel.

'He only kept me because of my black fur. And even then he would say horrible things about me being a mongrel because I had tabby blood in me.'

Atticus had never particularly thought about what sort of cat he was. Of course, he knew that some breeds of cat like Persians and Siamese were pure-breeds. Mimi was one – she was a Burmese. But he'd never met anyone who thought it mattered. Cats were cats. Who cared what type you were? He put his paw reassuringly on top of Bones's.

'My poor mother never recovered,' Bones said. 'Two months later, when I was fully weaned, she died.'

Atticus felt like crying himself. It was the saddest story he'd ever heard. Even sadder than the mermaid's.

'I think the Captain would have had me killed

too once he got a chance to replace me, but I took to the sea,' Bones continued. 'I learnt to sail and to navigate by the stars. The pirates showed me how to tie knots and read charts. I could climb up the rigging faster than any of them and hoist the Jolly Roger. They liked me,' she said simply. 'And the Captain's luck continued, so he kept me on. He got richer and richer and greedier and greedier. He found sunken ships full of treasure. He raided boats and stole people's money. As time went on he decided that I was indispensable – that I must be his new lucky charm after all. He's too stupid to know that you make your own luck in life.'

It was true. Atticus had never really believed in magic or lucky charms, except the mermaid of course. Call it what you wanted: luck, fate, destiny even – like the ship. Mimi was right: life was about making the right decisions and learning from the wrong ones, like the one he'd made about the beard-jumper competition. He was starting to think he'd misjudged Bones. Maybe she did have a good reason for what she'd done after all. Or at least maybe she thought she did.

'The two pirates I got on with best were

Herman Tucker and Fishhook Frank,' Bones said. 'They'd seen what Black Beard-Jumper did to my brothers and sisters and they didn't agree with it. They were kind. They brought me food and told me stories about countries I'd never seen. Black Beard-Jumper never let me ashore, you see, in case I tried to run away, like my mother.'

Atticus tried to imagine what it would be like to be stuck on a ship your entire life. He shivered. It was his idea of misery.

'One night they told me they were going to leave. They said they were going to find a ship and go after treasure more valuable than anything Black Beard-Jumper had stolen. They asked me if I wanted to come with them. I suppose they saw from my reaction that I did. We took one of the lifeboats and rowed away from the *Golden Doubloon* back to shore. They bought a boat and set sail to find the casket.' She paused. 'You know about the legend of the mermaid?'

'Mr Tucker told us,' Atticus said.

Bones nodded. 'From the port we sailed to the island we've just come from. Fishhook had an idea that was the starting point. He and Mr Tucker made the little wooden cabin in the clearing and a nice bed for me inside it. I used to go out hunting and fishing while they prepared for the voyage, and bring them things for tea. Eventually we set sail.' Bones's eyes were bright. 'We had some adventures, I can tell you. Those man-eating plankton are a bunch of trouble!'

Atticus swallowed. He didn't like the sound of them at all.

'Well, anyway, to cut a long story short, we got as far as the sea guarded by the giant lobster. Then that terrible thing happened to Mr Tucker's leg. We had to turn around.'

'What, back through the man-eating plankton?' Atticus queried.

'No.' Bones shook her head. 'The magical sea creatures don't disturb you if you sail *away* from the mermaid. There are no storms or hurricanes either. A few days later we dropped Mr Tucker off at the hospital on the mainland. He said once he was better he would return to Britain to be a fisherman. He said he wanted to settle down and get married.' She smiled. 'I'm glad he did. Mrs Tucker seems nice.'

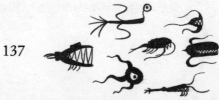

'She is,' Atticus confirmed. 'She used to be a secret agent called Whelk.'

'Oh!' Bones looked startled. 'I didn't know that. You don't think she knows I chewed the cables, do you?'

'Probably,' Atticus said gloomily. 'She always seems to know when I've done something wrong. Why *did* you chew the cables, anyway?'

'I'm coming to that,' Bones said. 'After Mr Tucker left, Fishhook wanted to complete the voyage to find the casket. But I'd had enough of the sea. And I was worried about what might happen if we actually did find the mermaid. Once Mr Tucker had gone, Fishhook started behaving strangely. All he could talk about was treasure and being rich and all the things he would ask the mermaid for once we found her. I thought he was becoming more and more like the Captain . . .'

'So you left?' Atticus guessed.

'Yes, I thought I'd be fine on my own. But I got into trouble for stealing food. The police came and put in me a cage and called me a stray. They took me to a place with a lot of other cats. That's where the Captain found me. He reckoned his luck had changed without me. That wasn't really it, though. He just didn't want anyone else to have me. He took me back to the *Golden Doubloon* and clapped me in irons for a week. He said if I ever tried to escape again, he would kill me like he'd killed my brothers and sisters. Worse still, he said that he would seek out Herman Tucker and Fishhook Frank and kill them too. I had no choice. I had to stay and do what he told me.' She looked at Atticus appealingly. 'I was frightened.'

'I don't blame you,' Atticus reassured her. And he didn't. Not any more. Whatever Bones's reason for chewing the cables, it wasn't because she was loyal to Black Beard-Jumper. 'That pirate's a brute.'

'Of course, Captain Black Beard-Jumper knew about the legend of the casket. But he didn't know that Herman and Fishhook Frank had gone looking for it. And none of us knew that Fishhook had finally discovered it after all these years until the Captain found out he hadn't been invited to this year's World Beard-Jumper Competition . . .' She paused. 'Was that when he cursed poor Inspector Cheddar?'

'Er, yes.' Atticus shifted uncomfortably. He

didn't want to get into the whole cursing thing with Bones.

'I thought so,' Bones said. 'Anyway, as soon as the Captain returned to the ship, he set sail to find Fishhook. He didn't tell anyone else about where we were going. He said he didn't trust any of the other pirates. Only Pam.'

'Pam?' Atticus repeated. 'Who's Pam?'

'Pam's his parrot.' Bones grimaced. 'She's a nasty piece of work. The Captain thinks she's clever because she can speak English. But I don't like the way she's been behaving recently. Not since those other birds arrived.'

'What other birds?'

'I can't remember what they're called.' Bones frowned. 'They look a bit like seagulls. Only they're black and white. Toothless Tony got them from a melon seller in an Egyptian bazaar by mistake. He was supposed to buy parrots.'

A melon seller? In an Egyptian bazaar? With black-and-white birds? For real? Atticus could hardly believe it. 'Their names wouldn't happen to be Jimmy, Thug and Slasher, would they?' he said grimly.

15

Bones stared at Atticus in astonishment. 'How do you know?' she exclaimed.

'I'll tell you another time,' Atticus promised. 'It's a long story. They're magpies, by the way. Thieving, scheming, cheating magpies.' He frowned. 'Do you think they know about the casket?'

'I wouldn't be surprised if Pam told them,' Bones said thoughtfully. 'She's pretty close with the boss one – Jimmy.' She giggled. 'I think she fancies him.'

'She must be nuts!' Atticus joked. He was thinking hard. If Jimmy knew about the casket, he'd be planning something with Thug and Slasher. The magpies would want to summon the mermaid before anyone else did. And Atticus was pretty certain one of their first wishes would be revenge on him!

'Well, it didn't take us long to find the island,' Bones carried on with her story. 'I don't think the Captain had been there before but I remembered it from the first time with Fishhook and Mr Tucker.' She shivered. 'I went ashore with the Captain and some of the pirates. Fishhook tried to run when he saw who had come to rescue him. But he didn't get far. Captain Black Beard-Jumper tied him up while the pirates searched the little log house. The Captain wanted to know if Fishhook had made a treasure map. The Captain didn't believe him when he said he hadn't. All pirates make treasure maps, he said. He was all for running Fishhook through with his cutlass there and then, but Fishhook said if he did that he might never find the casket. The Captain didn't want to waste any more time. So he took Fishhook back to the ship.'

'And left you?' Atticus guessed.

'Yes. My instructions were to stay on the island and keep a look-out. If I found a map, I was to destroy it. But I couldn't find anything. I'm not as

142

clever as you, Atticus. I still don't know how you did it.'

Atticus shrugged modestly. 'It was nothing,' he murmured.

'I'm sorry Michael thought it was me who found the map,' Bones added. 'You should have got the credit.'

'It's okay.' Now he knew Bones's history, Atticus could forgive her almost anything. One thing was still puzzling him though. 'Why did you follow us? And why didn't you come out of the jungle when you saw it was Mr Tucker?'

'I wanted to,' Bones said. 'But I couldn't. That's where my real loyalty lies, you see, Atticus: to Herman Tucker. I thought if Mr Tucker didn't find anything, he might give up and go home, where he'd be safe. If he went on and tried to find the casket and Fishhook, Black Beard-Jumper might kill him. I would have destroyed the map if I'd found it, to save him. Only you got there first. And that's why,' she said finally, 'I destroyed the computer equipment instead.' She looked at him wistfully. 'I still thought Mr Tucker might turn back if he couldn't radio for help.'

So that was it. She was trying to help Mr Tucker. She *was* loyal to him, after all. Atticus had been wrong. 'He can't turn back,' Atticus said simply. 'None of us can. The only way to cure Inspector Cheddar is to find the mermaid. We've got to go on. All of us.'

'I understand now,' Bones said. 'They're your family. You'd do anything to help them. You're loyal to them. That's what I feel like about Mr Tucker. He's the only good thing I know.'

'Not now he isn't,' Atticus said. 'You know me. And the Cheddars. And Mrs Tucker.' He felt as if a great weight had been lifted off his shoulders. Of course he wouldn't leave Littleton-on-Sea. He must have been mad to even think about it. Mimi was right. The children didn't blame him for what had happened. Nor did Mrs Cheddar or Mrs Tucker. They weren't like that. They loved him. And he loved them.

Loyalty: it was really important. Most cats didn't understand it properly. They liked their independence. But Mimi understood it. And so did Bones. And now he did too. Being part of the Cheddar family wouldn't just stop once he'd saved

Inspector Cheddar from the curse of the black spot. It was something that would last for the rest of his life.

'You're safe now, Bones,' he said. 'Once this is all over you must come back with us to Littleton-on-Sea. You'd like it there. Mr Tucker has a boat. You can meet the kittens.' Atticus grinned at the thought. 'They're loads of fun.'

'Thanks, Atticus,' Bones said gratefully. 'You've been so kind about all this.' She hesitated. 'Is there anything I can do to help you in return?'

'As a matter of fact there is,' Atticus said. 'You can teach me to sail. I've got a feeling we're going to need two ship's cats where we're going.'

145

Somewhere up ahead the *Golden Doubloon* had hit the Sea of Calamity. The pirates scurried to and fro across the deck in the darkness trying to keep control of the ship as the wind strained at the sails and the rained lashed at them like a whip.

Captain Black Beard-Jumper stood at the helm shouting commands. Pam sat on his shoulder keeping a watch on the men. Beside the Captain stood Fishhook Frank. His hair was long and his beard-jumper ragged from his time marooned on the island. His hands were tied behind his back. His expression was surly. Every now and then the Captain would bark a question at him. If he didn't reply Pam would fly at him angrily and peck him on the nose until he talked.

'Ready to go about!' the Captain yelled.

The pirates ducked as the boom swung across and the ship changed tack. They took up their new positions as the ship crested the next wave and plunged into a trough.

The magpies huddled beside some crates that had been lashed to the deck, trying to keep out of the way.

'Are we nearly there yet, Boss?'

Thug had his head over the side of the bucket in case he threw up. This time the bucket was full of pirate sick not dirty water. It kept sliding from side to side.

'No!' came Jimmy's muffled reply. His wing was spread across his face to keep out the spray. He separated a few feathers and poked his beak out so he could talk to the others. 'I already told you: this is the Sea of Calamity. After that we've got to navigate the Whirlpool of Doom, the Storm of Stupefaction and the Ocean of Terror.'

'What's that again?' Slasher had a turn at the bucket.

The ship listed suddenly. The bucket overturned, trickling sick along the deck. Thug trod in it.

'For goodness sake!' Jimmy fluttered on to the top of the crates. He wriggled his tail under the tarpaulin. 'The Ocean of Terror is where the man-eating plankton, the giant squid and the giant lobster live,' he shouted. The wind whistled through his feathers.

'Oh yeah.' Slasher joined Jimmy on the crate. 'Then there's Volcano Island. Fishhook Frank told the Captain the casket's there, right?'

Jimmy said nothing.

'Help!' Thug was flapping frantically. Every time he tried to land on the crate next to Slasher the wind pushed him off again. Eventually he managed it. 'Move up!'

The three birds nestled under the tarpaulin. A disgusting smell of sick wafted up from Thug's feet.

'Whereabouts on Volcano Island?' Slasher asked, resuming their conversation.

'I don't know,' Jimmy snapped.

'What do you mean you don't know?' Slasher frowned. 'I thought Pam told you everything.'

148

Since the arrival of Fishhook Frank on board the *Golden Doubloon*, Jimmy's information had been coming freely from Pam on a daily basis. Until that morning.

Thug chortled. 'Your girlfriend got the hump with you, has she, Boss? Is that why she's in such a bad mood?'

The magpies watched as Pam took another nibble at Fishhook Frank.

'Yeah, what's happened, Boss?' Slasher asked. 'You two had a row?'

'She wants to get married,' Jimmy said sourly.

'Married?' Thug repeated. 'What, you and Pam?'

'Yes,' Jimmy said. 'Me and Pam.'

Thug and Slasher fell about laughing. 'Chaka-chaka-chaka-chaka-chaka!'

'Shut up!' Jimmy tried to punch them both in the crop. It didn't work very well in the cramped space under the tarpaulin but it still hurt.

'Sorry, Boss,' Thug wheezed. 'What I meant to say was congratul-hations!'

'Yeah, many happy returns.' Slasher tried to shake Jimmy's wing.

Jimmy kicked him in the shins.

'I love weddings!' Thug gushed. 'Can I wear a hat?'

'We could have worm cake!' Slasher said enthusiastically. 'With beetle-shell sprinkles.'

'And confetti!' Thug gasped. 'I love that stuff! It's all pretty, like snow.'

The two magpies were beginning to warm to the idea.

'Can we invite some baby blackbirds to scare?' Slasher begged.

'Can we have a knicker trampoline?' Thug pleaded.

'There's not going to be a wedding,' Jimmy snapped.

Thug and Slasher exchanged looks. It was always important to read Jimmy's moods correctly, especially if you didn't want to be pushed into a puddle of pirate sick. They tried a different approach.

'I can't say I blame you,' Thug said. 'She's horribly ugly. Her face looks like she's been run over by a steam roller.'

'Yeah and she's got a bum like Wally's,' Slasher said, remembering their old friend. Wally's turbocharged poo-packed bum was legendary amongst the magpie gang. 'Imagine having to share a nest with that!'

Thug grimaced. 'Nasty, Slasher my friend,' he agreed. 'Very nasty.'

'The problem is,' Jimmy said dismally, 'if I don't marry her, she won't tell me where the casket is.'

Thug and Slasher glanced at one another. A bit like the ship, Jimmy's mood had changed direction again.

'Looks like you'll have to do what she wants, then, Boss,' Slasher spoke hesitantly. 'If that's the only way to be certain we'll get to the mermaid first. I mean, we don't want to take any risks.' He nudged Thug.

'She's not that bad,' Thug said generously. 'Apart from the way she picks her beak and eats her own droppings.'

Jimmy shuddered.

'I'd marry her myself,' Slasher said, 'only she hates me.'

'Look at it this way, Boss,' Thug said wisely, 'once you've summoned the mermaid you can ask for what you want, right?'

'Right,' Jimmy said cautiously.

'So the first thing you ask her for is to send Pam to prison . . .'

'Or Patagonia,' Slasher suggested.

'Yeah, whatever that is,' Thug agreed. 'Get rid of her anyway.'

'I suppose so,' Jimmy said.

'Then the next thing you ask for is one of them lovely sunny holidays in the Caribbean with your mates,' Slasher said.

'Maybe,' Jimmy agreed gruffly.

Slasher winked at Thug. They were talking him round!

'With lovely fluffy towels and a beautiful lady magpie singing to you under the stars,' Thug sighed. 'Chaka-chaka-chaka-chaka-chaka.'

For a moment the magpies forgot about the wind and the heaving of the boat and the dreadful smell coming from Thug's feet. They imagined they were on holiday in paradise.

'That would be nice,' Jimmy admitted.

'And a five-star tree-house hotel with a catskin on the floor . . .' Slasher said softly.

'I can see it in my head, Boss,' Thug sighed. 'It's

got brown and black stripes with four white corners, and a red bit in the middle made out of a handkerchief.'

'Atticus Claw,' Jimmy said dreamily.

'If only!' Thug sighed.

'I wish!' Slasher nodded.

'Maybe,' Jimmy said.

'It's not like you even have to go through with it,' Slasher tried again.

'Yeah, you can say you want one of them long hen-gagements,' Thug said. 'And then get the mermaid to dump her somewhere before the wedding.'

That decided it.

'Okay,' Jimmy said. 'I'll go and tell her now.'

17

Atticus had the wind in his whiskers. He felt proud of himself. He had improved so much at sailing since Bones came on board that Mr Tucker had even asked him to take the wheel again. And it was fun, too.

Bones was a good teacher. She taught him how to hoist the sails and change direction safely without knocking Inspector Cheddar overboard. She taught him how to tie knots and operate the winch. It was through Bones that Atticus discovered that a halyard was the rope that hoisted the sail and a sheet was the one that controlled it. She explained that the best way to avoid seasickness was to look at the horizon. Best of all she showed him how to dangle a line over the side and catch fresh sardines. Atticus had never tasted anything as delicious as those fresh sardines. He didn't think he could have a better friend than Bones.

'It's good to see you two getting along so well,' Mrs Tucker remarked.

Atticus purred.

'Aye,' Mr Tucker said. 'You make a grand crew.'

Atticus glowed with pride.

Mr Tucker checked his charts against Fishhook Frank's map and glanced at the horizon. 'By my reckoning we'll be at the Sea of Calamity in no time.'

'Do you think we'll get to the mermaid before Black Beard-Jumper does?' Mrs Tucker said in a low voice. 'The kids are really worried about their dad.'

Atticus was too. It was Tuesday: only three days now until the curse was expected to strike. Inspector Cheddar had taken to his bunk to write poetry. He had a permanent air of melancholy about him. He didn't even seem cross with Atticus any more, which was usually a sign that he had something else on his mind.

'I's not worried about that,' Mr Tucker reassured her. 'I's reckons Black Beard-Jumper's only a day's sailing ahead of us. And we's got the advantage of a smaller ship.' His eyes twinkled. 'Besides, if we plan it right, we can use the *Golden Doubloon* as a decoy once we get to the Ocean of Terror.'

'What do you mean, Herman?' Mrs Tucker asked. She offered Atticus some cat biscuits. He took them gratefully. The kids were right. Sailing was hungry work when you did it properly. Even cat biscuits tasted good.

'Those pirates stink like a heap of camel dung,' Mr Tucker explained. 'The man-eating plankton will smell 'em a mile off. Once they swarm on board and start gnashing, it'll be each man for himself. The *Doubloon* will begin to wallow. That's when the lobster and the squid will strike. With any luck the whole ship will go down. Them what's left will have to take to the lifeboats. Meanwhile we sneak past and get to Volcano Island ahead of them.'

Atticus thought that sounded like an excellent plan. He'd started having nightmares about the man-eating plankton chomping at his fur and nipping his whiskers.

Bones dropped down lightly on the deck beside him. 'Look,' she said.

Atticus raised his eyes. The sky was darkening. It was getting foggy. Ahead of them a series of white-capped peaks stretched into the distance. 'Is that land?' he asked, puzzled.

'No, Atticus,' Bones replied cheerfully, 'they're waves. That's the Sea of Calamity. We're nearly there.'

Atticus could hardly believe it. The waves were like mountains, each one higher than the last. The *Destiny* would never get through it.

'Don't worry, Atticus,' Bones whispered. 'We'll be all right. Just remember what I've taught you.'

'Tell the children to stay below,' Mr Tucker ordered.

Mrs Cheddar did as she was bid.

'Right, crew,' Mr Tucker said in a businesslike voice. 'You know what to do. Get to your stations. Clip yourselves on.'

The five of them took up their positions on the ship. They clipped on their safety lines.

'Here goes!'

They had reached the Sea of Calamity.

The ship began to climb the first wave. Atticus's duty was to man the jib; the smaller of the two triangular sails. It fluttered as the wind caught it the other side. This time Atticus knew what to do. He loosened the rope, waiting for Mr Tucker's order. They had nearly reached the pinnacle of the wave.

'Ready about!' Mr Tucker yelled. Everyone ducked.

The jib boom swung across. The sail filled with wind. The ship lurched forward. Atticus fastened the rope. Mrs Tucker and Mrs Cheddar gave him the thumbs up. They were on the mainsail, doing the same thing. Bones was scurrying about, keeping things shipshape.

'Hold on!'

The ship pitched down the other side of the wave on its new tack.

Atticus didn't have time to feel afraid. One by one, waves rolled towards the ship, each one higher than the last. He battled with the jib as the ship tacked this way and that, trying to keep the movements of the sail under control, heaving on the rope until his paws were raw. The sea was like a rollercoaster. Up and down they went. It was hard to know which was worse: the perilous climb to the top of the wave with the towering water about to break over them, or the fearful lurch in the pit of Atticus's stomach when they crested the wave and the boat began to fall.

They battled on and on, Mr Tucker at the helm roaring encouragement when their spirits began to fade.

Finally, after what seemed like hours, the waves subsided. The mist cleared. They found themselves sailing once again on a smooth flat sea. They had survived the first obstacle. The Sea of Calamity was behind them.

'Well done, Atticus!' Bones said. 'You can have a break now.'

'Thanks!' Atticus padded towards the cabin. His muscles felt weak. His legs were wobbly. Bones bounced after him. It was amazing how much energy she had! All Atticus wanted to do was lie down on a comfy bed and have a long sleep. But he knew there wasn't time for that. The Whirlpool of Doom was only minutes away.

'Good work, crew!' Mr Tucker congratulated them from the cockpit.

Michael and Callie were waiting for them below. Their faces were white.

Mrs Cheddar hugged them. So did Mrs Tucker.

'It's all right,' Mrs Cheddar said. 'Everyone's safe. How's Dad?'

'Terrible,' a voice groaned. Inspector Cheddar staggered into the cabin with his notebook.

Atticus looked at him in alarm. Inspector Cheddar's eyes were bulging. His face was green. 'Can anyone think of a word that rhymes with verruca?' he asked plaintively.

Atticus felt Bones put a paw on his shoulder. 'Don't worry, Atticus, it's just seasickness. If it was the curse of the black spot his eyeballs would have exploded by now.'

'Oh, er, thanks,' Atticus meowed. 'That's good to know.'

Just then, he heard a familiar cry. 'All hands on deck!' It was Mr Tucker.

'The Whirlpool of Doom,' Bones announced. 'Come on!' She raced up the cabin steps to join Mr Tucker. Atticus chased after her with Mrs Tucker and Mrs Cheddar.

'Can't we help, Mum?' Callie begged.

'No,' Mrs Cheddar said firmly, 'it's too dangerous. Batten down the hatches and look after Dad.'

Michael closed the cabin doors.

Back on deck, the five crew members clipped themselves back on.

They were just in time. The sea was churning. Not up and down like it had been before. This was even worse. Atticus couldn't get his balance. The ship yawed from side to side. It was as if they were caught in a giant washing machine. It was all he could do to keep his footing.

'It's pulling us in!' Mr Tucker shouted.

To his horror, Atticus could feel the sea tugging at the boat. He glanced upwards. The two sails were full of wind. The boat should be going forwards! But it wasn't. An invisible force was pulling it in the opposite direction.

'Over there, Atticus.' Bones was beside him. 'Look.' She pointed to the stern.

Atticus stared. There was a huge hole in the sea behind them!

'It's the whirlpool!'

Atticus could hardly believe his eyes. Spirals of seawater rippled towards the hole, like a pattern on a shell. The nearer they got, the choppier the water became. Around the edge of the hole the sea swirled in angry torrents. He had never seen anything so terrifying in his life before.

'We need more sail!' Mr Tucker shouted. 'Quick! It's taking us down.'

The ship was being drawn closer to the seething whirlpool. Atticus could feel it starting to move in slow circles of its own. The ship couldn't compete with the power of the sea.

'I can't hold her!' Mr Tucker wrestled with the wheel. The ship twisted and groaned. 'Edna, hoist the spinnaker! I'll try and get her downwind.'

'I can't, Herman! It's all we can do to hold the mainsail!' Mrs Tucker and Mrs Cheddar hung on grimly to the ropes. 'If we let go now, we're finished.'

'Bones!' Mr Tucker shouted in desperation. 'You and Atticus will have to do it.'

Atticus felt himself freeze. The spinnaker was the big balloon-like sail at the front of the boat. It was one thing hoisting it on a calm sea in nice weather. This was something completely different. 'Don't worry, Atticus, you can do it.' Bones set off along the deck to secure the pole. Atticus struggled after her.

Atticus held the bag while Bones wrestled with the colourful sail, wrapping her body round it so that it didn't fly away. Atticus looked on as she clipped it expertly to the ropes. It flapped and tugged in the wind, nearly throwing her off. 'Pull on the halyard!' Bones cried. 'I'll take the sheets. We need to trim it just right or we might lose it.'

Atticus understood what she meant. Trimming the sail meant allowing it to fill with just the right amount of wind at just the right moment. Bones had to keep the wind out of the spinnaker until it reached the top or it might get twisted around the mast.

'Okay, go!' Bones dropped down on to the deck and raced back to the cockpit.

Atticus heaved at the rope. His back paws slid along the deck.

'Use the winch!' Bones shouted.

Atticus grabbed the winch handle. He fixed it into the socket and took hold of it in his front paws. He began to turn the handle.

'Keep going!'

Atticus's muscles screamed with pain. It wasn't that the winch was stiff. It was the effort of keeping his balance as the ship plunged about in the boiling sea. But he did as Bones told him. The spinnaker inched up the mast, flapping like a crazy bird. He glanced back. The whirlpool was getting nearer. The ship was being drawn in. He gritted his teeth and pushed on.

Finally the sail reached the top of the mast.

Atticus collapsed, panting on the deck. He could feel the ship circling towards the whirlpool. He saw Bones secure the first of the two sheets with a winch. Then she leapt across to the other side of the cockpit and grabbed the other. She held the sheet loosely in her paws, her tail high so that she could tell the direction of the wind. She would have to get it just right. Atticus saw her tail twitch; her body stiffening as she tightened the sheet.

BOOMPH! The spinnaker filled with wind. It ballooned out in a great billow of colour.

Atticus felt the ship leap forward. It shot away from the churning edge of the whirlpool. It zipped through the shell-like spirals and out into clear water.

The two cats embraced. 'We did it, Atticus!' Bones said, her eyes shining.

Atticus breathed a sigh of relief. For the time being anyway, they were safe!

To Jimmy's horror, Thug's advice proved to be wrong. Pam the Parrot had insisted on getting married as soon as possible.

'We can't!' he protested. 'There's no one here who can do it. We need a vicar or something.'

'Oh no we don't, Jim!' Pam contradicted. 'The Captain is licensed to perform wedding ceremonies at sea. Let's do it before we get to the Ocean of Terror.'

As soon as the *Golden Doubloon* had passed safely through the Storm of Stupefaction, Pam dragged Jimmy to the Captain's cabin and closed the door.

Thug and Slasher looked on through a windowpane. Captain Black Beard-Jumper was sitting at his desk. Pam fluttered up to his shoulder and started to squawk something in English. The Captain let out a huge roar of laughter. Then he put on a solemn face and stood up.

Pam flew down to the floor, gripped Jimmy in a wing-lock and hoicked him on to the desk.

'This is it!' Slasher said excitedly.

'I never got to wear a hat,' Thug sighed.

'It wouldn't fit you anyway, not with the way your feathers are all puffed out,' Slasher consoled him.

Thug's head looked twice as big as normal. So did his body.

'I feel all jingly-jangly,' he complained. 'Since I got hit by that bolt of lightning in the Storm of Stupid.'

'The Storm of Stupefaction,' Slasher corrected him. 'Not the Storm of Stupid.'

The *Golden Doubloon* had navigated the storm intact, all except for Thug.

'Stupefaction means getting whacked so you don't know what's going on, like what you did,' Slasher explained. 'Whereas stupid just means dumb, like what you *are*. D'you get it?'

'No,' said Thug

Inside the cabin, Captain Black Beard-Jumper

166

reached in his pocket and produced a metal bird ring. He held it out to Jimmy.

Jimmy took it reluctantly. Pam thrust her gnarled foot towards him. Jimmy slipped the ring over her scaly talons with difficulty.

'By the power invested in me as the Captain of the *Golden Doubloon*, I now pronounce you magpie and wife!' Captain Black Beard-Jumper proclaimed. 'You may kiss the bride.'

Pam puckered up. Jimmy looked as if he was about to be sick.

'Eerrrggh.' Slasher shivered. 'I feel sorry for the Boss.'

'Me too.' Thug pulled a face. 'Imagine kissing that! I'd rather kiss Wal's bum.'

'I hope that mermaid fixes her good and proper,' Slasher said.

The ceremony over, the Captain threw open the door and strode out, his big boots clomping along the deck.

Thug and Slasher flew round to the cabin door to greet the happy couple.

All they could hear was squawking. It was Pam.

'Don't give me any more of your excuses, Jim,

get up there and mend the crow's nest,' Pam screeched.

'What's got into her?' Thug whispered.

'I dunno,' Slasher replied.

'And when you've done that there's a mirror to hang in our hatch. Make sure you get the hook in the right place. And then there's my poo bucket to clean. I can't poo in a dirty bucket.'

'Why can't you clean your own poo bucket?' Jimmy snapped back.

'I'm busy!' Pam squawked. 'Now get on with it!' Pam flew off after the Captain.

Jimmy paced up and down the cabin, muttering to himself.

'All right, Boss?' Slasher said nervously.

Jimmy gave him a filthy look. 'I should never have let you talk me into this. All she does is nag, nag, nag. She only wanted to get married so I'd do all her jobs for her.' He advanced on Thug, his eyes glittering. 'This is your fault. You said we could have a long engagement.'

'Not far to go now though, Boss, until we get to

168

Volcano Island,' Thug said hastily. 'Then the mermaid can mash her.'

'With any luck she'll get mangled by the man-eating plankton first,' Slasher said. 'Did she tell you where the casket is?' He hopped sideways out of Jimmy's way.

'Not yet,' Jimmy said bitterly. 'She's saving it for our wedding night.'

'That's tonight, Boss!' Thug exclaimed.

'I know, you dimwit!' Jimmy pecked his tail.

Just then there was a shout from the brig. The foghorn sounded.

They were approaching the Ocean of Terror: the most dangerous part of the voyage so far.

The magpies hopped outside the cabin.

'Where is everyone?' Thug wondered.

The *Golden Doubloon* was eerily silent. The only noise was the slop-slap of gentle waves hitting the bow, and the groaning of the sails as the wind pushed them slowly towards their destination.

'On watch,' Jimmy said shortly. 'Look.' The pirates stood around the ship's rail. Each and every man had his eyes focused on the sea. Most of them had their cutlasses at the ready. A few had drawn pistols. They were watching for the man-eating plankton.

'I reckon we'll be safer higher up.' Jimmy flew up into the rigging towards the crow's nest. Slasher and Thug fluttered after him. They perched in a line peering down at the men below.

'I don't like this,' Thug whispered.

'Neither do I,' Slasher cawed softly.

The foghorn sounded again.

FONK! FONK! FONK!

All of a sudden the ship was enveloped in thick yellow mist.

'What happened?' Thug squawked.

'I can't see!' Slasher sobbed.

The two magpies clung to one another, shivering with fear.

Down below there was a shout from one of the pirates, followed by a scream.

CHOMP. CHOMP. CHOMP.

CHOMP. CHOMP. CHOMP.

The magpies strained their ears. 'Is that chewing I can hear?' Jimmy said uncertainly.

The sound of an enormous belch penetrated the fog.

'It's the man-eating

plankton!' another pirate yelled. 'They're coming aboard.'

There was pandemonium amongst the pirates.

Shots rang out. Cutlasses swished through the air. The screams were interspersed with swearing.

'Hold steady, you lily-livered poltroons!' Captain Black Beard-Jumper roared at his men. 'Or you'll cut each other to ribbons. STAMP ON THE BEASTS!' His big boots clattered on the wooden deck. It sounded like he was dancing a jig.

Other pirates followed his lead.

TAP TAP TAP TAP!

CHOMP CHOMP CHOMP CHOMP!

BBUUUURRRRPPPP!

The cacophony of noises went on and on. It was impossible in the fog to know what was happening or who was having the better of it – the man-eating plankton or the pirates. From the amount of burping going on, it sounded like the man-eating plankton were.

'Chaka-chaka-chaka-chaka-chaka!' Up in the rigging Thug's beak started to chatter. 'I don't want to be eaten alive!' he screamed. 'I'm too young to die!'

'Shut up, you idiot!' Jimmy hissed. 'The plankton don't know we're up here.'

'Er, I think they do now, Boss,' Slasher said.

The sound of chomping became louder. Tiny pinpricks of green were forging their way up the rigging towards the magpies in an advancing tide.

'Should we fly away, Boss?' Slasher gulped.

Jimmy looked around desperately. 'We fly away in this and we might never find the ship again!' The fog was thicker and yellower than ever, like dirty cotton wool.

'What are we gonna do?' Thug screeched.

Just then there was a flutter of wings. Pam landed beside them.

'You hang that mirror yet, Jim?' she nagged.

'Not quite, Pamela, my dear,' Jimmy said hastily. 'It's next on my list!'

'Yeah? Well, I brought you this, for when you get to the poo bucket,' Pam produced a packet from under her arm.

THUMPERS'
SCRUBBIT

'Never mind your poo bucket, you demented dodo!' Thug screeched. 'We're about to be devoured by man-eating plankton!'

Pamela nipped Thug hard on his head.

'Don't call me a demented dodo,' she said, 'or I'll get the cook to pluck you.'

'We do have a situation, though, er . . . darling,' Jimmy said.

The man-eating plankton were getting perilously close.

'Blimey!' Pam peered down at the advancing hordes. 'I didn't realise they could climb.' She shook the packet of Scrubbit. 'I reckon if it works on my poo bucket, it might work on these little beasts. Whadayousay we give it a try, Jim?' She tore open the packet with her beak and sprinkled it on the swarming plankton.

The man-eating plankton started to cough. Some of them began to retreat. Others dissolved into green gunk.

Pam sprinkled more Scrubbit.

More man-eating plankton fell away.

Pam shook the packet of Scrubbit again. It was empty.

'Blast it! I'm out!' Pam swore.

'Now what?' Slasher's beak was chattering. 'Chaka-chaka-chaka-chaka-chaka!'

A new wave of plankton had come into view. It was like a green blanket edged with a great wall of yellow teeth.

'Fishhook Frank says that's why they attack in the fog,' Pam regarded them with interest, 'so you can't see their gnashers.'

CHOMP CHOMP CHOMP.

CHOMP CHOMP CHOMP.

The man-eating plankton were closing in fast again.

'I can't afford to lose any more tail feathers!' Thug screeched. 'Help!'

'Come with me.' Pam led them up to the crow's nest. 'I've got an idea.'

She jumped on to the edge of the basket and lowered her tail.

PHUT! PHUT! PHUT!

PHUT! PHUT! PHUT!

Pam let out a deluge of droppings, followed by an explosion of foul-smelling gas.

Thug fainted.

The man-eating plankton stopped in their tracks.

PHUT! PHUT! PHUT!

PHUT! PHUT! PHUT!

'Take that you little blighters!' Pam screeched.

There was a fizzing noise, then a series of faint pops.

POP! POP! POP!

POP! POP! POP!

Slasher peered over the edge of the crow's nest. 'Pam's poop is making them explode!' he said in awe. 'Wow, Boss, I don't envy you having to clean out her poo bucket.'

Jimmy looked wan.

'That'll teach you!' Pam screamed at the rest of the retreating plankton. She turned to Jimmy. 'I'm going back to see how the Captain's doing! Wait here until he gives the all-clear. Then go and fix that mirror.'

The magpies waited anxiously in the crow's nest, except Thug who lay unconscious, his feet in the air.

A few minutes later Captain Black Beard-Jumper's voice bellowed through the fog. 'All right, you horn-swaggling scumbags, the show's over.

Collect the bodies and throw them overboard.'

The fog began to lift.

Jimmy and Slasher peered down.

The deck was littered with human skeletons. Splashes of blood were plastered all over the deck and on the sails.

''Ere, Thug, have a look at this! It's well gruesome!' Slasher propped him up.

Thug opened his eyes.

'I'm not mopping that up,' he said, before he fainted again.

'Phew,' said Jimmy. He began to preen his glossy feathers. 'That was close.'

'Pam did well,' Slasher said, slapping Thug around the face. 'You glad you married her, Boss?'

'Of course I'm not,' Jimmy spat. 'I'd rather be eaten by a giant squid.'

Just then the ship gave a terrible lurch.

The magpies tumbled on to the deck.

All the pirates started screaming again.

'Maybe you shouldn't have said that, Boss,' Slasher gulped.

Waving in the air above the *Golden Doubloon* were eight enormous tentacles.

19

On board Mr Tucker's ship, *Destiny,* Atticus was on watch. 'Bones!' he called. 'Look! It's the *Golden Doubloon!*'

The pirate ship was just visible in the distance. It was the first time Atticus had seen it. It was like something from a movie. The huge hull rose tall and black out of the water, topped with four masts and a mass of billowing sails. No wonder Bones was such a good ship's cat!

'Wait!' he whispered. 'What's wrong with it?' The ship was lurching from side to side. 'And what are those?' He pointed to the eight thick white limbs that enveloped it.

Bones glanced at the stricken *Doubloon.* 'It's the giant squid,' she said quietly. Then she raced downstairs to alert Mr Tucker.

Of course! Atticus watched in horror as the squid took hold.

Soon the whole crew of *Destiny* was assembled on deck. All except Inspector Cheddar, who remained below. He was still trying to think of a word that rhymed with verruca.

They watched in silence for a few minutes. Mrs Tucker lowered her binoculars. 'Maybe it is a good thing you used to be a pirate after all,' she told her husband. 'Otherwise we wouldn't have got this far.'

'Thanks, Edna.' Mr Tucker looked pleased.

Atticus didn't know what to think. On the one paw if Mr Tucker *hadn't* been a pirate then he would still be in Littleton-on-Sea doing police-catting with the kittens; Inspector Cheddar wouldn't have been cursed, and the kids wouldn't be worried their dad was about to die. On the other paw he wouldn't have met Bones and learnt to sail. Atticus sighed. Life could be very confusing sometimes, the way things happened when you didn't expect them to.

One thing was certain though: Mr Tucker was

the best person to get them safely to Volcano Island. Atticus had no doubt about that. They had come unscathed through the Storm of Stupefaction, and so far they had navigated the Ocean of Terror without incident. The magical sea creatures had been drawn to Captain Black Beard-Jumper's ship just as Mr Tucker had predicted, leaving the *Destiny* to sail through easily. Best of all they had made good progress. There was one day to go until sunset on Friday. If everything went according to plan they would just be in time to save Inspector Cheddar from the curse of the black spot.

'We'll lie low for a bit,' Mr Tucker said. 'Then, once we're sure the *Doubloon*'s sunk, we'll push on.'

Atticus glanced at Bones. 'Are you okay?' he said. He wondered how she felt now that the ship she had spent almost all her life on was in trouble.

'Couldn't be better,' Bones said briskly. 'It serves Black Beard-Jumper right. I just hope Fishhook makes it. He's the only one who doesn't deserve to drown.'

Atticus couldn't blame Bones for not feeling sorry for the pirates' plight: not after what Black Beard-Jumper and his men did to her family. He wondered how the magpies were faring. Knowing Jimmy and his gang, Atticus decided, they were bound to find some way of escaping the giant squid's clutches. Jimmy was the most devious animal he'd ever come across, apart from Ginger Biscuit.

Callie was casting nervous glances at the sea. 'How do we know the plankton won't come after *us*?' she said in a small voice.

'They's full up with pirates,' Mr Tucker said. 'That's how.'

Atticus felt relieved: he'd been worrying about that too.

A terrible crack echoed across the Ocean of Terror. One of the squid's tentacles had broken the *Golden Doubloon's* main mast.

'Here you go, Atticus!' Mrs Tucker held the binoculars to his eyes. Atticus could see the pirates swarming about the deck, trying to gather in the remaining sails. Some of them shot at the giant squid with pistols. Others attacked it with cutlasses.

The more they swiped, the angrier the squid became. Its tentacles lashed at the ship.

'What about the giant lobster?' Michael asked. 'Where's that?'

'It'll be lurking on the seabed beneath the *Doubloon*,' Mr Tucker said gloomily. 'Planning its attack. That's what it did with me, anyways. I was so busy trying to outrun the squid, I didn't notice the lobster until it grabbed me with its crusher claw.'

'There it is!' Mrs Cheddar cried.

Atticus saw the huge pink crustacean haul itself up the side of the *Golden Doubloon*. Its eyes bulged. Its antennae waved frantically in the air as it guided itself towards its victims, its two monstrous claws nipping at anything that got in its way. Atticus shuddered. He didn't think he'd ever want to eat shellfish again.

The pirates jabbed at the lobster with their swords.

'They's won't get nowhere doin' that,' Mr Tucker commented. 'It's got a shell as thick as a pirate's arm.'

'They're lowering the lifeboats!'

181

Mrs Tucker snatched back the binoculars. 'Black Beard-Jumper must have given the order to abandon ship.'

Atticus could see the lifeboats flop into the water beside the doomed vessel. Men hurried down the ladders and threw themselves into the boats. The *Golden Doubloon* was listing dangerously to her port side. The giant squid wrapped its tentacles around the prow. Another crack rang out.

'She's done for!' Mr Tucker announced.

The ship gave a terrible groan. Then slowly it began to sink.

The remaining pirates jumped overboard and swam for their lives. There was only one figure still visible on the ship.

'It's Black Beard-Jumper!' Mrs Tucker said. She gave Atticus another look down the binoculars.

'Why doesn't he leave?' Atticus meowed at Bones.

Captain Black Beard-Jumper stood tall and proud, his cutlass raised above his head, his beard-jumper curling down his chest.

'A captain should go down with his ship,' Bones replied. 'It's traditional.' She shrugged. 'Black

Beard-Jumper won't let himself drown though. He's just showing off to his men. He wants that casket.'

The giant lobster was making its way towards the Captain who swiped at its antennae with his sword. The lobster stopped, confused: just long enough to give the Captain the chance he needed. With a shout of defiance he grabbed hold of a loose rope and plunged over the side of the *Doubloon* into a lifeboat.

'Told you,' Bones said.

The pirates picked up the oars and the lifeboat pulled slowly away from the stricken ship.

Mr Tucker nodded, satisfied. He emptied his pipe over the side of the boat and took hold of the wheel. 'We's got the advantage now,' he said. 'I's reckon we'll be at Volcano Island by first light. It'll take them a week to row there. Let's go.'

Atticus resumed his place beside the jib.

The rest of the crew took up their stations. This time the children were allowed to remain on deck.

Atticus scanned the horizon to see if he could see any sign of Volcano Island.

He blinked.

Something was poking out of the water. For a horrible moment Atticus thought it might be one of the giant squid's tentacles. He stared at it.

It wasn't a tentacle. It was a grey metal tube, twisted over at the top. It finished in a round aperture like an eye. He swallowed. It was as if the object was staring back at him from the sea.

'What is it, Atticus?' Bones asked.

'Over there.' Atticus pointed, but the tube had disappeared. He shook his head. 'I don't know . . . I thought I saw something,' he mumbled.

'Probably a bit of driftwood,' Bones suggested. 'It's easy to imagine things when you've been at sea a long time.' She bounced off.

Atticus busied himself with the sheet. Bones was probably right – he was imagining things. But he couldn't get the idea out of his head that while they were watching Black Beard-Jumper and the pirates, something else had been watching them!

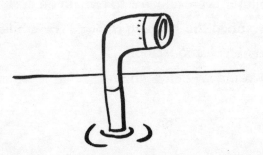

'Land ahoy!'

Atticus was dozing in the cabin when the shout finally came from Mr Tucker that they were nearing Volcano Island. The crew had been taking it in turns to get some rest before the final part of the journey, except Bones, who never seemed to be tired.

Atticus checked the calendar. It was Friday – the thirteenth day of the seventh month: the day the curse was due to strike. It had taken them longer than Mr Tucker had expected to reach their destination. There were only a few hours to go until sunset.

He jumped off Mrs Tucker's bed and scrambled up to the deck.

Volcano Island lay before them.

It was conical in shape – just as Fishhook Frank had shown it on the map. Its summit was shrouded in smoke. A red vein of lava trickled from its peak, zigzagging its way down the rocky face of the mountain towards the sea. In contrast to the island where Fishhook Frank had been marooned, there was no beach and no vegetation: only rock.

Mr Tucker was chewing his pipe stem anxiously.

'What's the matter?' Atticus asked Bones.

'There's nowhere to land,' Bones replied.

'We'll get as close as we dare in the ship,' Mr Tucker told the crew. 'Then we'll have to motor in on the rib and see if there's somewhere to moor.' He and Bones began to lower the dinghy over the side of the ship.

This time Atticus didn't need a bag to hoist him into it. Bones had taught him how to climb up and down the rigging using his four paws. He whizzed down the ladder after the children. The rib sat low in the water with everyone in it, especially as Mrs Tucker insisted on bringing a big, heavy plastic container with her at the last minute.

Atticus secretly hoped it was full of packed lunch. A cat had to eat, even in times of emergency!

The sea was as smooth as glass. They sped over the water with barely a bump.

Volcano Island loomed towards them. The closer they got, the craggier the rock face appeared. Great boulders rose from the sea around the base of the island. Behind the boulders the sheer cliffs of the volcano towered above them.

Atticus felt apprehensive. It looked impossible to get close to the island even in the dinghy, let alone find a way in through the rock to the lagoon under the mountain.

Mr Tucker consulted Fishhook Frank's map.

'There should be a path leading into the mountain,' he said, scrutinising it.

Atticus remembered now. The path led into the mountain under a waterfall of lava.

'We need to be nearer to the lava flow.' Mrs Tucker pointed to the trickle of red.

Except it wasn't a trickle any more, Atticus observed. This close in, it was more like a torrent.

They motored towards it. The air temperature grew hotter. And the smell was disgusting! Atticus wrinkled his nose. It was like rotten eggs!

'It's sulphur, Atticus.' Michael coughed. 'It's a

187

gas that comes out of volcanoes when they erupt.'

'Everyone keep their eyes peeled for the path,' Mrs Tucker ordered. 'And cover your nose and mouth.'

They all held something to their face to keep out the stinking gas. Atticus used the flap of his neckerchief, holding it with one front paw while he balanced on the other. Mrs Tucker gave Bones a scarf.

The rib chugged on slowly. The boulders were packed tight. They were never going to get past them!

All of a sudden an opening appeared.

'I'll bet it's this way,' Mr Tucker slipped the rib cautiously into the opening. The boulders crowded either side of the little inflatable boat.

Atticus thought it might be a dead end but after a short while they edged out from between the boulders into a narrow channel next to the sheer face of the cliff.

'I thought so,' Mr Tucker said in a satisfied voice. 'Now we's getting somewhere. Watch out for submerged rocks!' he added. 'We don't want to sink like the *Titanic*.'

188

Atticus had heard of the *Titanic*. It was a big boat that hit an iceberg under the water and sank to the bottom of the sea. He didn't want that to happen either. He stared fixedly ahead, looking for hazardous rocks (and icebergs, just in case).

They inched forward. Atticus's ears were buzzing from the effort of concentrating amidst the heat and smell the lava was giving off. His eyes stung. It was hard to breathe. The sulphur seemed to clog his lungs. It was even worse than the smoke from Mr Tucker's tobacco pipe.

Suddenly Mr Tucker cut the engine. 'I's can't take us any closer,' he said. 'The rib will melt!'

The air was scorching now. Even the sea was hot, like a bath. Steam rose gently from its surface. They were still about fifty metres from the lava flow.

'But where's the path into the mountain?' Mrs Cheddar said despairingly. 'I can't see it anywhere!'

Atticus couldn't see it either. He scanned the mountain, forcing his watering eyes to focus, tracing the lava's path as it descended. The lava followed the fissures in the rock, clinging to every crevice until it reached a point about thirty metres above the sea where a ledge jutted out horizontally beyond the boulders beneath. From there the lava dropped vertically into the sea in a glowing red wall.

It was definitely the waterfall of lava shown on Fishhook Frank's map. But where was the path into the mountain? There were no steps or footpath hewn into the rock. There was no opening in the cliff face. And even if there had been, Atticus thought, you'd fry if you went that close to the tumbling lava.

'I'm doomed,' Inspector Cheddar sobbed. 'Doomed!'

Mrs Cheddar and Mrs Tucker exchanged worried looks.

'Fishhook Frank must have found the way in!' Michael said bravely. 'Or he wouldn't have known about the underground lagoon. The path must be here somewhere!'

'It's no good!' Inspector Cheddar gulped back a sob. He got out his notebook and started to scribble some more poetry. 'Can anyone think of anything that rhymes with lava?' he asked plaintively.

Nobody could. Atticus wished Inspector

Cheddar would think of easier words to rhyme with, like 'cat'.

'We can't give up now, Dad!' Callie hugged him. She looked appealingly at Atticus. 'Help us, Atticus,' she whispered. 'Please! Can't you use your instinct or something?'

Could he? Maybe. It was definitely worth a try. His instinct had helped him before when he didn't know what to do. Atticus tried to relax and let it take over. *What possible way was there to pass beneath a waterfall of fire?* Only water could protect you from fire . . .

Wait! Atticus felt his fur prickle with excitement. That was it!

Bones was watching him carefully. 'What is it, Atticus?' she meowed.

'Water!' he purred joyfully. 'We're surrounded by it! The path into the mountain must be through the sea! Otherwise, how could the mermaid have got in?'

'Of course!' Bones exclaimed. 'She couldn't walk. She could only swim!'

Now the cats knew what they were looking for, they squinted again at the wall of rock behind the ledge, lower this time, where the rock met the ocean.

'There!' Atticus nudged Bones. A small cave lay directly beneath the ledge, further along the narrow channel. Seawater sloshed in and out of the opening.

Atticus started pawing at Mrs Tucker's sleeve.

Bones meowed frantically.

Mrs Tucker grabbed the binoculars.

'Holy coley!' she hissed. 'Atticus has found the way in!' She passed the binoculars round so everyone could see. 'Look! Through the cave.'

'But it's full of water!' Mrs Cheddar said doubtfully.

'Think about it, Mum!' Michael's puzzled expression suddenly lifted. 'The mermaid must have swum in . . .'

'So maybe we have to as well!' Callie finished for him.

Atticus purred like a tractor. Children *were* clever, like cats.

'Of course!' Mrs Cheddar threw her arms around her husband.

'One slight problem,' Inspector Cheddar sighed,

biting the end of his pen, 'how are we going to get there if we can't take the boat?' He frowned. 'What rhymes with *Titanic*?'

'We'll use these.' Mrs Tucker removed the lid of her waterproof box and drew out a blue rubber suit, flippers, a pair of goggles, some breathing apparatus and a small metal tube marked OXYGEN. 'I've brought one for everyone, including Atticus and Bones. The suits are made of neoprene so they'll withstand high or low temperatures.' She glanced up. 'Well, don't look so surprised,' she said when she saw everyone was gawping at her. 'I did use to be a secret agent, you know. We all had these. It was standard issue.' She handed out the kit.

Atticus watched closely. Of course it was a good idea of Mrs Tucker's to bring neoprene diving suits for everyone just in case there was an emergency, but he'd been hoping for a fish-paste sandwich.

'I brought these as well to give us energy.' Mrs Tucker rummaged in her box. She handed round bottles of water and cereal bars. 'And this is for you, Atticus. Share it with Bones. She gave him a bowl full of chopped sardine.

Atticus munched his helping of sardine gratefully and washed it down with a drink of water while Bones did the same. Mrs Tucker was a remarkable human, he decided. She really did think of everything.

'That should hold her.' Mr Tucker secured the rib by tying a rope around a point on one of the craggy boulders while Callie zipped Atticus into his suit. It felt surprisingly cool, considering how tight it was. Maybe neoprene was a bit like fur, he thought. It kept you cool when it was hot and hot when it was cool.

Atticus was amazed how calm he felt. Swimming! Him! A cat! But he wasn't just any cat, he reflected, as Michael fixed goggles over his eyes and flippers to his back paws. He was Police Cat Sergeant Atticus Grammaticus Cattypuss Claw. And he no longer hated the sea, thanks to Bones, although he was still afraid of sharks.

Callie giggled. 'Atticus and Bones look like seals!' she laughed.

Atticus didn't mind. Everyone else looked pretty silly too. Like penguins!

'What you have to remember, Atticus, is to breathe through your mouth,' Bones told him as Mrs Tucker held out the breathing apparatus.

'You mean you've done this before?' Atticus asked.

'Fishhook Frank taught me to snorkel,' Bones said. 'This is the same thing only deeper. Really, it's beautiful down there once you get the hang of it.' She gestured at the ocean.

'Okay, I'll try.' Atticus tried not to panic as he felt the rubber mask grip his nose. He took a few shuddering breaths through his mouth. The sulphurous air tasted foul. He felt himself choking.

'Use the breathing tube. In and out. Nice and steady,' Bones told him.

Atticus sucked on the mouthpiece. In and out. Nice and steady. His breathing slowed. The air tasted better, and he felt like he was getting enough oxygen.

'Good.' Mrs Tucker nodded, satisfied. 'Okay, team, let's find that casket.'

The rescuers slid off the side of the rib into the steaming water.

Atticus dithered on the edge.

'Come on, Atticus, we'll look after you.' Michael held out his arms.

'Promise!' Callie said.

Atticus closed his eyes and jumped in with a splash.

21

Swimming, Atticus decided, was surprisingly easy once you got the hang of it. No wonder fish liked it so much. He thought he might try and teach Mimi when he got back to Littleton-on-Sea.

And the ocean was beautiful! They were swimming along the narrow channel between Volcano Island and its ring of rocks about two metres below the surface. The water was as clear as diamonds. The sea teemed with fish of every different colour and variety. Some had funky stripes. Others had glossy spots. Some shone like rainbows with delicate fins that trailed in pretty ribbons from their backs. Atticus had never seen anything like it. Even the rocks were coated with dazzling colours. Turquoise fronds and bright yellow sponges nestled together with what looked like small trees made of broccoli, only they came in pink and orange and purple, instead of green.

As they swam towards the lava waterfall, the sea became warmer and warmer. Curiously it didn't seem to affect the sealife. If anything it got more stunning the warmer it became. Atticus was glad they didn't have to breathe the air. That close to the lava flow the smell must be unbearable.

Callie and Michael were up ahead of him with Inspector and Mrs Cheddar, Mr Tucker and Bones. They were making good progress. Inspector Cheddar was in the lead. He was swimming as if his life depended on it, Atticus thought. Then he remembered – his life did depend on it! Mrs Cheddar turned and beckoned, then swam off again. Atticus followed as quickly as he could. Managing flippers was tricky. He was glad Mrs Tucker was behind him. Whenever he got muddled up Mrs Tucker's firm hand on his rear gave him a strong push forward.

They were close to the cave entrance now. Atticus could see the opening in the submerged cliff face. It was a lot bigger than he had imagined – a great cavern which descended as far as he could see into the depths of the ocean. Atticus felt nervous. It was almost as if it didn't have a bottom at all – as if it went all the way to the centre of the earth. Maybe, he thought anxiously, that was where all the magical sea creatures lived: where they went when they had devoured anyone who threatened the mermaid. He looked about for signs of the man-eating plankton. He tried not to think about them nipping at his fur with their huge teeth.

They swam into the cave and on towards the centre of the mountain. FLIP, FLAP, FLIP, FLAP. The sunlight above them faded. Everything was darker, colder, scarier. Atticus could hardly see. FLIP, FLAP, FLIP, FLAP. All Atticus could hear was the gentle swish of flippers and the strange echo of his breath in the mouth tube. He could barely make out the Cheddars. Mr Tucker and Bones had disappeared. He was sure something was lurking in the water, watching them. He kicked on. FLIP, FLAP, FLIP, FLAP, FLIP, FLAP.

Gradually the light became stronger again: the water became clearer. Atticus relaxed a little.

Mrs Cheddar pointed upwards.

It was weird being under water, Atticus reflected. Everything seemed to happen in slow motion. Mrs Cheddar started swimming towards the surface. The rest of the group followed her.

POP! Atticus's head emerged out of the water beside Callie's and Michael's and Bones's. He looked about.

'We did it, everyone!' Mrs Tucker popped up beside him and removed her mouthpiece. 'We made it to the lagoon!' She helped Atticus out of his breathing apparatus and goggles. He took in a lungful of air. The air was pure. It smelt of flowers. He took in another lungful, glad to be free of the sour stink of the volcano.

'Wow!' Callie gasped.

'It's beautiful!' Michael breathed.

Atticus looked around in astonishment. He had thought the sea was amazing but the lagoon was out of this world!

The lagoon was cut out of rock. Waterfalls (real ones, made of water not lava) tumbled into it from high above. The biggest white flowers Atticus had ever seen wound their way on dense creeping vines up the face of the rock towards the roof of the volcano. Tiny birds hovered in the air collecting nectar. Delicate butterflies fluttered to and fro. Atticus listened, entranced. You could hear their wings beat!

'Where's the light coming from?' Callie asked in awe.

'There are light tunnels,' Michael pointed upwards. 'Look.'

Atticus gazed up. High above them the rock was studded with light, like a night full of bright stars.

'The tunnels must lead to the outside,' Michael said. 'That's how the light gets in.'

'There!' Inspector Cheddar exclaimed suddenly. 'There she is! The mermaid!'

Atticus looked round.

A little way away, at the base of a waterfall, was the mermaid. She was lying on a rock, flapping her tail gently back and forth in the water, admiring herself in a mirror and brushing her long blonde hair.

Atticus blinked. He eyed the mermaid warily. This wasn't at all what he had expected. *Where was the casket? And why wasn't the mermaid asleep?*

'Isn't she supposed to be in a casket?' Callie whispered.

Atticus purred. That was exactly what he was thinking.

'Casket, basket!' Inspector Cheddar cried. 'Who cares!! She must have woken up after her thousand-year nap and let herself out for a swim.'

He pulled himself out of the water in his neoprene suit and shot off, leaping and bounding athletically across the rocks, like Bones.

Atticus frowned. Something didn't feel right. Fishhook Frank's map didn't say anything about the mermaid letting herself out for a swim. X marked the spot. It showed the casket in the middle of the lagoon under the volcano. With the mermaid presumably still in it, asleep. He squinted across the lagoon but he couldn't see anything. The casket would be under the water, where the mermaid could breathe. She couldn't survive for long out of the water. That's how the old woman had managed to trick her in the first place.

'I don't like this,' Atticus meowed to Bones.

Mrs Tucker didn't either. She was staring intently

at the mermaid. 'Hmmmm,' she said. 'I wonder
. . .' She didn't say what she wondered. She started
after the Inspector. 'Let's take a closer look. Come
on.'

The rest of the party followed, picking their
way carefully over the rocks, except Bones who
bounded across like a gazelle.

Up ahead, Inspector Cheddar had already reached
the mermaid.

'Magic mermaid on the shore, please grant me
what I'm wishing wish for!' he yelled ecstatically.
Finally he would be free of the curse! His eyeballs
wouldn't explode after all! He wouldn't get the
squirts or the shakes, the lumps, the bumps or the
camel humps. Inspector Cheddar felt so happy at
that moment, he was even prepared to forgive
Atticus.

The mermaid didn't appear to have heard him.
She carried on brushing her hair.

'Magic mermaid on the shore, please grant me
what I'm wishing for!' Inspector Cheddar repeated.

The mermaid turned round and glared at him.

Inspector Cheddar started. The mermaid was as ugly as a troll! Her face was all wrinkly and the skin round her neck and elbows sagged like a plucked chicken. He wished she was wearing something more than a shell bra and a tail. He wondered if it would be rude to offer her his neoprene suit.

'Vot do you vant?' the mermaid demanded.

Inspector Cheddar grimaced. The mermaid didn't just have an ugly face, she had a horrible voice as well: like a frog with tonsillitis.

'I've come to ask for a wish,' he said impatiently.

'Vell I vish you hadn't,' the mermaid said. 'I'm all out of vishes today.'

'You mean someone got here before I did?' Inspector Cheddar said aghast.

'Yeah, big bloke vith boots, an eye patch and a long beard.' The mermaid scratched her armpit. 'Or it might have been a jumper.'

'Captain Black Beard-Jumper!' Inspector Cheddar groaned. 'I'm doomed! Any minute now I'm going to get the curse of the black spot!'

'Vell don't give it to me,' the mermaid said. 'Or Biscuit,' she added softly.

'Biscuit?' Inspector Cheddar repeated. 'Who's Biscuit?'

The mermaid grinned. Her teeth were black. 'You remember Biscuit,' she said. 'He's furry, vith big teeth. Likes rats. Come here, my orange angel of darkness.'

A large ginger cat stepped out of the shadows and joined the mermaid on the rock.

'Wait a minute!' Inspector Cheddar said. There was something familiar about the mermaid. And he'd definitely seen the cat somewhere before. 'Have you been to Egypt recently?' he asked suspiciously.

The mermaid didn't reply. Instead she reached up with one bony hand and pulled off her long blonde wig. Beneath it was a grizzled mat of grey hair, bristling with sharp-looking hairpins.

Inspector Cheddar recognised the mermaid now. He'd already been on the receiving end of those hairpins on more than one occasion. 'Klob!' he gasped. 'It's you!'

'Surprise!' The mermaid said.

ZIP! A hairpin flew through the air towards Inspector Cheddar and hit him in the leg. He toppled to the rock, snoring.

Bones was the first to reach the scene. She looked at the mermaid in confusion.

'Bones!' Atticus meowed desperately. *Klob and Biscuit!* What were they doing here?! 'Be careful! It's a trap!' But Bones was too far ahead. She couldn't hear him.

ZIP! A second hairpin flew towards Bones. She collapsed beside the Inspector, fast asleep.

'Dad!' Callie screamed.

'Bones!' Mr Tucker howled.

'I knew it!' Mrs Tucker muttered. 'I had a feeling Klob might turn up.'

'Biscuit,' Klob shouted. 'Ve've got company.'

Ginger Biscuit growled. POP. POP. POP. POP. He popped out his claws one by one as the rescuers approached.

Atticus ducked down out of sight. If Klob and Biscuit got control of the mermaid it was almost worse than if the pirates did! Without thinking, he crept behind a vine and hid amongst the flowers.

Mrs Cheddar ran to her husband. 'You witch!' she screamed at Klob. 'How could you?'

'Dad, wake up!' Michael started shaking him.

'He von't vake up,' Zenia Klob said in a bored voice. 'I put extra super concentrated sleeping potion on my hairpins today.'

'How did you get here, Klob?' Mrs Tucker demanded.

'Easy,' Klob answered. 'I took a submarine. Much qvicker than sailing.'

Atticus listened from behind the flowers. A submarine! That was what he had seen from the ship yesterday. A periscope from a submarine! Klob must have followed the pirates when they bought the magpies. And sailed after them in the submarine to the Ocean of Terror. But how had she beaten the *Destiny* to the lagoon? Atticus scratched his ear, puzzled. *How did Zenia Klob even know there was a lagoon?!! Or a mermaid?!!! Let alone how to find it?!!!! Apart from themselves, only Fishhook Frank and Captain Black Beard-Jumper knew that* ... Atticus felt his fur stiffen with fear. *Oh no!* He wanted to cry out: to warn Mrs Tucker and the Cheddars, but if he did, then he would be discovered and he wouldn't be able to help them escape from what he sensed was about to happen.

'Vere's Atticus?' Zenia Klob asked suddenly.

207

'Only, Biscuit vants to chew him.'

Atticus froze. They mustn't give him away!

The children glanced at one another.

'He's on the ship,' Michael said.

'He hates water,' Callie added.

Atticus breathed a sigh of relief. He should have known he could rely on the kids!

'Of course,' Zenia said. 'Poor little Atticus. Doesn't vant to get his fur all vet. I'd forgotten he's such a cowardy cat.'

Atticus didn't care what Zenia Klob said about him. As long as she believed he was on the ship, they still had a chance.

'You're under arrest, Klob,' Mrs Tucker said grimly. 'You're wanted by Interpol.' She advanced on Zenia Klob and Ginger Biscuit .

'Nice try, Agent Velk,' Zenia Klob said. 'But I think you'll find you're outnumbered.'

'Outnumbered?' Mrs Tucker repeated. 'How? I don't get it.'

Atticus did. He waited, wriggling as far as he could into the vine.

'Biscuit!' Zenia Klob clapped her hands. 'Get Captain Black Beard-Jumper and the pirates!'

22

Captain Black Beard-Jumper emerged from behind the rocks. He was followed by the surviving pirates and a man in raggedy clothes. His hands were tied together behind his back with rope.

'Fishhook Frank!' Mr Tucker exclaimed.

'Herman Tucker!' Fishhook shouted with relief.

'Very touching, I'm sure,' Captain Black Beard-Jumper snarled. 'You can go to Davy Jones's locker together.' He pushed Fishhook Frank towards Mr Tucker and prodded a boot at the sleeping Bones. 'With this traitorous mongrel.'

Atticus's whiskers twitched with fury.

'Leave her alone!' Mr Tucker shouted. He scooped Bones up in his arms so the Captain wouldn't hurt her.

Atticus's eyes moved back to the Captain. Upon Captain Black Beard-Jumper's left shoulder sat a large green parrot. *Pam,* Atticus thought. Sitting beside her was Jimmy Magpie. Atticus's eyes narrowed. It was just as he expected: Jimmy had wheedled his way in with Pam the parrot, so he could be the first to get to the mermaid and say the rhyme.

'CHAKA-CHAKA-CHAKA-CHAKA.'

The chattering came from a wicker cage carried by one of the other pirates. Atticus squinted at it. Thug and Slasher were inside. At least they wouldn't be any trouble. It was Jimmy he was worried about, and Biscuit. He could see Ginger Biscuit padding about, his yellow eyes searching for something. Atticus swallowed. *Ginger Biscuit was looking for him! The kids might have fooled Zenia, but Biscuit knew he was out there somewhere.*

'Think you could outsmart the greatest pirate in the world, did you, Tucker?' Captain Black Beard-Jumper roared. 'By leaving us to die on the Ocean of Terror? Well, unluckily for you we had help, see?' He nodded in Zenia's direction. 'Ms Klob brought us here in the good ship *Submarine*. Came

210

under Volcano Island we did. But not before we blasted the sea creatures with the latest Russian underwater bomb so they can't do no more nibbling and munching and drowning.' He grinned. 'We beat you to it, Tucker. You and your friends have lost.' He consulted his watch. 'Half an hour to go until sunset.' He glanced at Inspector Cheddar. 'Not long now until this hornswoggling weasel be struck by the curse.'

'Hooray!' the pirates sang. There was no TV on the *Golden Doubloon* so watching someone being struck by the curse of the black spot was what counted for good entertainment on a long voyage at sea.

'Now, let's be waking the mermaid,' Black Beard-Jumper said.

All eyes turned to the lagoon.

Stretching out across the water, Atticus could see a series of smooth dark stones. And beyond that, in the centre of the lagoon, something twinkled.

Captain Black Beard took out his eyeglass. 'The glass casket,' he said rapturously.

'Let me see!' Zenia Klob wriggled out of her

mermaid tail. She snatched the eyeglass from Captain Black Beard-Jumper. 'Magic mermaid on the shore, please grant me vot I'm vishing for,' she chanted softly. 'Vot shall ve vish for first, Biscuit? How about a lovely banquet of rat and pike-head stew?'

Captain Black Beard-Jumper snatched the eyeglass back. He glared at Zenia Klob.

'It be me that's doing the wishing,' he roared. 'Not you.'

Atticus peered out. This was his chance: whilst the villains were arguing he could race across the stepping stones and summon the mermaid himself! He squeezed his way behind the vines towards the stones.

'Vot?' Zenia Klob said menacingly. Her hand reached towards her grey mat of hair. She pulled out a fistful of hairpins. 'No vun tells Zenia Klob, Russian mistress of disguise, vot to do.'

'Threaten the greatest pirate who ever sailed the sea, would you?! I'll have you flogged, you turncoat,' the Captain shouted. 'Men! Seize her!'

The pirates closed in on Zenia Klob.

ZIP! ZAP! Hairpins flew everywhere.

Atticus hesitated. He couldn't risk making a

break for the stepping stones now. He might get hit by one of Zenia's poisoned hairpins. And if the pirates saw him, they'd cut him to ribbons with their cutlasses. *And where was Biscuit*? He had disappeared from Zenia's side.

'I'll get you for this!' Zenia gasped as the pirates tied her hands behind her back like Fishhook Frank.

'Tie up the others!' Captain Black Beard-Jumper ordered.

The pirates did as they were bid. Only Bones and Inspector Cheddar remained free, and they were both asleep.

'Right, men, let's go.'

Captain Black Beard-Jumper made his way towards the stepping stones.

Atticus got ready to spring. He still had the element of surprise. He could dodge past the pirates and get to the mermaid before they realised what was happening. He tensed his back legs, watching for his opportunity.

Captain Black Beard-Jumper lifted his boot towards the first stone. Suddenly Pam whispered something in his ear. He stopped: his boot in mid-air. 'Get Fishhook Frank,' he ordered.

Atticus wondered what was wrong. He waited.

The pirates man-handled Fishhook Frank towards the stepping stones.

'Why didn't you cross it?' Captain Black Beard-Jumper grabbed Fishhook Frank by the hair and held his cutlass to his throat. 'When you had the chance before? You got this far. Why didn't you summon the mermaid yourself?'

It was a good question, Atticus thought. Fishhook Frank must have reached the lagoon the last time, otherwise he couldn't have made the map. *So why didn't he finish the job?*

'I wanted to,' Fishhook Frank said miserably. 'But I was too afraid, even after everything I'd been through to get here, all those years of searching. I had a feeling something was watching me. Something in the water. Something terrible that I couldn't see.'

Funny. Atticus had had that feeling too, when they swam through the cave.

'What sort of thing?' Black Beard-Jumper demanded.

'I don't know,' Fishhook Frank said hopelessly. 'It was just a feeling. I believed I would die if I crossed the stones. I was too scared to go on. It felt like the place was cursed. That's why I turned back.'

'The sea creatures all be dead now,' the Captain ruminated. 'I saw them being bombed with me own eyes not three hours ago.' He dropped Fishhook Frank, satisfied. 'Come on, men. There's nothing can stop us now!'

He began to pick his way across the stepping stones, the other pirates following.

'What are we going to do?' Mrs Cheddar said despairingly.

Atticus glanced up towards the roof of the volcano. The light was fading slightly. The sun would be setting soon.

'Can anyone think of anything that rhymes with curse?' Inspector Cheddar spoke in his sleep. 'Apart from hearse.'

'Don't give up, Dad!' The children begged.

'Atticus will save you,' Callie whispered. She looked around the cavern. 'I know he will.'

'So do I,' Michael said. 'Because he's the best cat ever.'

Atticus felt his heart glow with pride. They still believed in him! He couldn't let them down.

'Atticus is here?!' Zenia looked astonished. Then she snorted. 'He von't save your dad,' she sneered. 'Biscuit vill kill him first.'

Atticus took a deep breath. It was all up to him now. He had about fifteen more minutes to save Inspector Cheddar's life.

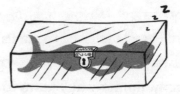

23

Atticus emerged from his hiding place and padded cautiously across the rocks towards the stepping stones. There was still no sign of Biscuit.

The pirates strung out in a line across the stones, picking their way carefully from one to the next, their eyes focused on the casket. At the head of the line was Captain Black Beard-Jumper. He only had a few more stones to negotiate before he reached the mermaid. Pam and Jimmy were still on his shoulder. Atticus saw Jimmy Magpie flex his wings, getting ready to fly. He was relieved to see Pam give Jimmy a hard peck on the head. Pam was keeping her beady eye on Jimmy. Jimmy would have to wait until the very last minute if he didn't want Black Beard-Jumper to pot him with his pistol.

Atticus crept forward to the lagoon. He leapt on to the first stone. Then the next. And the next. The pirates hadn't seen him. The stones were slippery. They were too busy concentrating on keeping their own feet to notice him. Atticus was beginning to think luck was on his side after all.

Just then he felt something pin his tail. Atticus struggled to escape but he couldn't. A large cat-shaped shadow spread across the stepping stone.

'Going somewhere?' a voice hissed.

'Biscuit!' Atticus tugged at his tail. Ginger Biscuit had it firmly by the claws. 'Let me go!'

'I knew you were here,' Biscuit said. 'Skulking about as usual.'

'Get off me!' Atticus yowled. 'I need to get to the mermaid.'

'Don't we all!' Biscuit laughed. 'And guess what my first wish will be? A nice slow cat-drowning. Yours,' he added unnecessarily. He flicked out the claws on his free paw.

POP! POP! POP! POP!

Biscuit's claw raked through the air towards Atticus's face. Atticus ducked.

'We don't have time for this!' Atticus yowled.

218

'Jimmy's up there with Captain Black Beard-Jumper. We need to hurry or he'll be the one who summons the mermaid. And it's not just me he wants revenge on, remember? He hates you too!'

Understanding dawned in Ginger Biscuit's eyes. He released his grip. 'I'll get you later, Claw,' he threatened. 'At least the mermaid will.' He leapt on towards the casket.

Atticus leapt after him.

Atticus had reached the line of pirates. He dodged between the first pirate's legs and leapt on to another stone, then another. One of the pirates swiped at him with his cutlass but Atticus barely noticed. He had to catch Biscuit and stop Jimmy! He got ready to take the next spring.

Just then something strange happened.

He felt the stone tilt beneath his paws. It began to rise out of the water. Atticus looked round in confusion.

Something odd was happening to all the other stepping stones too. The pirates had their arms out like aeroplanes to try and keep their balance as the stones bucked under their feet. Ahead of him, Ginger Biscuit was struggling to keep a pawhold.

'What's happening?' Captain Black Beard-Jumper shouted furiously.

One of the pirates gave an agonised cry. 'Stonefish!' He screamed. 'They're not stepping stones. They're stonefish!'

Stonefish? Atticus had never heard of stonefish. He looked down between his paws uncertainly.

The pirates began to curse. Some of them tried to turn and retrace their steps but the stones, or whatever they really were, bucked and reared, as if they were trying to shake them off.

SPLASH! Other pirates tumbled into the water.

'Run, Atticus!' Mrs Tucker's voice cut through the pirates' curses. 'Whatever you do, don't get stung! Stonefish are deadly. They're worse than snakes!'

Worse than snakes! Atticus bounced from one stonefish to the next, trying to touch each one for only a few seconds so it didn't sting him. Biscuit was still up ahead of him, but he was losing ground. The ginger cat's ears lay flat on his head as he crouched on a stone, not knowing whether to go on or back; water all around him. Atticus could tell he was terrified.

Only a short time ago Atticus would have felt the same. But he wasn't afraid of water any more. Not since he'd met Bones. And he didn't have time to be afraid of the stonefish. He had to save the Inspector.

One of the pirates passed Atticus in the other direction, heading away from the casket. The pirate jumped heavily on to the next stonefish. Suddenly he let out a terrible cry. His body became rigid. The pirate's face froze in an expression of shock. His flesh turned grey. His limbs stopped moving. Atticus gasped. The pirate hadn't just been poisoned. He had actually turned to stone! These stonefish were magical, like the other sea creatures that guarded the mermaid. Fishhook Frank had been right to be afraid!

'Careful, Atticus!' the children cried. 'Get off the stepping stones!'

Atticus jumped on to the stone pirate. The same thing was happening all around him.

One by one Captain Black Beard-Jumper's men were turning into statues as the stonefish poisoned them with their magic venom to protect the mermaid. A few of the statues toppled into the lagoon. Most simply stood there frozen in their positions of flight.

Atticus saw Ginger Biscuit float by on a piece of driftwood. He wouldn't be any more trouble. There was only Jimmy and Captain Black Beard-Jumper to go now.

Atticus jumped on to the arm of the next stone pirate, then on to the head of the one after that, making his way nimbly towards the casket without touching the venomous creatures that lay beneath the surface of the lagoon.

'CHAKA-CHAKA-CHAKA-CHAKA-CHAKA!' a familiar voice chattered.

Atticus started. *Thug?*

'It's that bloomin' cat again!' another voiced croaked.

And Slasher?

For one dreadful moment Atticus thought the other magpies had escaped. Then he saw that one of the pirate statues still held the wicker cage of magpies in his stone fingers.

'Watch out, Boss!' Thug screeched, poking his

head out between the bars. 'It's Claw!'

'Make sure you say the rhyme first, Boss!' Slasher screamed after him. 'Before Claw does!'

'I'm doing my best, you morons!' Jimmy squawked back. 'A little help would be appreciated!'

Up ahead on Black Beard-Jumper's shoulder, Pam had Jimmy by the tail feathers.

'CHAKA-CHAKA-CHAKA-CHAKA-CHAKA!' Jimmy was trying desperately to escape.

'Oh, no, you don't, Jim!' Pam squawked. 'That mermaid belongs to the Captain.'

'Leave me alone!' Jimmy screamed.

'I should have known you were no good when I first set eyes on you,' Pam lamented. 'I should never have agreed to marry you.'

Married?! Jimmy Magpie was married?! That was news to Atticus. He jumped on to the next stone pirate. He was closing fast now. Black Beard-Jumper was only three stepping stones ahead of him.

'Get off me you stupid parrot!' Jimmy kicked and struggled. 'I never wanted to marry you in the first place. I'd rather be eaten by a shark.'

The two of them tugged and fought.

'Er, Boss,' Thug's voice trembled. 'Maybe you shouldn't have said that.'

Atticus glanced at the lagoon in horror. A large grey triangular fin was making its way swiftly towards the stepping stonefish. The fin was at least twice the size of the one they had seen at the start of the voyage when Atticus had accidentally knocked Inspector Cheddar off the ship.

'Shark!' Slasher screeched.

'Help!' screamed Thug.

Atticus gritted his teeth. Only two more stones to go and he would reach Black Beard-Jumper and Jimmy. Two leaps from that lay the casket, twinkling brightly in the water. He took another leap, perching on the last stone pirate, getting ready for his final pounce. He couldn't make it to the casket in one go. There were two stones left. He'd have to go through Black Beard-Jumper's legs and risk the venom.

Captain Black Beard-Jumper struggled on to the last stone. It rocked and swayed beneath his huge boots. *Why hadn't he turned to stone like the others?*

Atticus wondered. Then he realised. The boots! They were so thick they must be protecting him from the venom.

'Claw!' Jimmy's glittering eyes turned on Atticus. They glowed with hatred and frustration. 'You can't win this time, you know.'

'You bet I can, Jimmy!' Atticus growled. 'Congratulations, by the way.'

'Pam, warn the Captain!' Jimmy cawed. 'The tabby wants the treasure.'

'CAT! CAT! CAT! CAT! CAT!' Pam screeched in the Captain's ear.

Captain Black Beard-Jumper turned to face Atticus. He raised his pistol.

Just then a ball of black fur hurtled past Atticus towards the Captain. 'Watch out, Atticus!' a familiar voice cried.

'Bones!' Atticus shouted. She must have woken up! All that energy had defeated Zenia's sleeping potion.

BANG!

The pistol let out a shot. It winged past Bones. Bones crumpled. The bullet had grazed her shoulder. She landed on the final stepping stone between Captain Black Beard-Jumper's boots.

'No!' Atticus yowled. He had to reach Bones before she turned to stone! Any second now and the stonefish would release its deadly venom again.

Atticus hopped lightly across to the last stonefish. Somehow he managed to throw Bones on to his back. Her body was light. 'Hang on, Bones!' A trickle of blood threaded down his whisker but he felt Bones's sinewy front legs clasp him round the neck.

Above him, Black Beard-Jumper slashed wildly at him with his cutlass, cursing.

Suddenly Atticus had an idea.

He popped out his claws and ripped the toe of Captain Black Beard-Jumper's boot where it connected with the sole. With his last ounce of strength Atticus leapt off the stonefish and on to the rim of the Casket of Desires.

BANG!

Captain Black Beard-Jumper let out another shot. It whistled past Atticus's whiskers. Then the Captain gave a cry of pain!

Pam began to shriek with grief.

Atticus glanced round. The venom had penetrated the rip in the Captain's boot. Captain Black Beard-Jumper had turned to stone: one arm outstretched with a stone pistol at the end of it, his mouth open in one last thunderous roar.

24

Atticus looked down at the casket. Through the clear glass lay the mermaid, asleep in the water of the lagoon. She was the most beautiful living creature Atticus had ever seen. Her auburn hair tumbled to her slim waist. Her skin was pale and delicate. Her green tail lay in a perfect curve. Her face was peaceful and serene: like Callie's when she was asleep.

'Open it, Atticus!' Mrs Tucker yelled from the shore.

'You can do it!' Mrs Cheddar called. 'I know you can!'

'Ow!' Inspector Cheddar mumbled. 'My eyeballs hurt!'

'Quick, Atticus, quick!' the children begged.

'The curse is starting.'

Atticus glanced up. The canopy of light was tinged with orange. It was nearly sunset.

Another trickle of Bones's blood dropped off Atticus's whiskers on to the casket.

He had to save Bones. He had to save Inspector Cheddar.

PING! Atticus pinged out his claws. Carefully, one paw at a time so as not to dislodge Bones, he made his way around the edge of the casket to its golden lock. The edge was wide enough for a cat to walk along comfortably, like the rim of a bath. Atticus felt relieved. At least he had plenty of room to work in.

He lay Bones down gently beside him and stared at the lock. Once, when nothing very much depended on it, he'd been the world's greatest cat burglar. But now that everything depended on it – ON HIM – he wasn't sure that he *could* do it any more. His claws already ached from where he had scratched a hole in Black Beard-Jumper's boots. But he had to find a way. He had to dig deep. Atticus took a deep breath to steady himself. Then he reached out a paw and began to fiddle with the lock. It wasn't hard, he saw to his relief. It was old. A thousand years old. Worn away by the salty sea.

The lock gave way with a clunk. Atticus sat back. Bones lay beside him. His paws were shaking.

Very slowly the lid began to open by itself.

'CHAKA-CHAKA-CHAKA-CHAKA-CHAKA!'

Somewhere behind him, Jimmy and Pam were still fighting. 'Get off me, you old hag,' Atticus heard Jimmy say. 'That mermaid is mine!' He felt the beat of wings. Jimmy had escaped!

'Say it, Atticus!' Mrs Tucker yelled. 'Before that blasted bird does.'

The lid of the Casket of Desires was nearly fully open.

'Magic mermaid on the shore, please grant me what I'm wishing for!' Atticus whispered.

Jimmy flew at him. 'CHAKA-CHAKA-CHAKA-CHAKA-CHAKA!'

'SQUAWK! SQUAWK! SQUAWK! SQUAWK!' Pam flew at Jimmy.

Atticus cradled Bones with one paw, swiping at the angry birds with another. It was too late now. There was nothing more he could do. Maybe the mermaid couldn't wake up. Maybe it was dead.

Just then the sea began to churn. The shark was back! Atticus could see its huge fin cutting through the water towards them. As it got closer it raised its head. Atticus caught a glimpse of its gaping mouth and row upon row of backward-pointing teeth. He closed his eyes. He hoped if he was going to die it would be quick.

There was a horrible chattering and squawking. Then a splash.

SNAP! SNAP! SNAP!

Atticus could hear the sound of the shark's teeth clashing together. He waited for his turn.

There was another splash, then silence.

Atticus opened his eyes. Pam and Jimmy had disappeared. So had the wicker basket containing Thug and Slasher. The shark was circling the lagoon slowly. But it didn't come near Atticus or Bones. He looked at the casket.

The mermaid's eyes were open. He'd done it! He'd summoned her! That was why the shark couldn't eat him. It was too late. He'd already said the rhyme.

The mermaid blinked at Atticus. Then she sat

up and looked around apprehensively. 'Where's the old lady?' she asked.

'She's not here,' Atticus said. 'Well, not that one anyway,' he added as he remembered Zenia.

'How did you find me?' the mermaid said sadly. 'The sea creatures said no one would.'

'I know, I'm sorry,' Atticus apologised. 'We came because we had to. It's my family. One of them's been cursed.' Quickly he explained about Inspector Cheddar and how Captain Black Beard-Jumper had cursed him with the mark of the black spot. 'And my friend, Bones,' Atticus said. 'She tried to help me, you see, and the Captain shot her.' Bones's breath came in short, ragged bursts. 'You're the only one who can save their lives, otherwise I wouldn't ask you for anything. I promise.'

The mermaid looked at him curiously. 'You mean you wish me to help others?' she said slowly.

'Yes!' Atticus felt a tear trickle down his cheek.

'You don't want anything for yourself?'

'No!' Atticus said. 'Nothing!' Right at that moment he didn't even want any sardines. All he wanted was for Inspector Cheddar and Bones to be cured.

232

The mermaid gasped. 'Then I'm free!' she said.

'What do you mean?' Atticus asked, bewildered.

The mermaid kissed him on the nose. 'Only the one who makes a selfless wish has the power to release me. And that's what you have done. Thank you, er . . .'

'Atticus,' said Atticus.

'Atticus,' said the mermaid. 'Lay your friend in the water beside me. Don't worry I won't let her drown.'

Atticus laid Bones next to the mermaid. The water lapped gently over her.

The mermaid lifted her hands to her face and blew into them. She placed them on Bones. Bones stretched. Then she opened her eyes. There was no sign of the wound. It had completely disappeared.

The mermaid picked her up and cuddled her. To Atticus's amazement Bones's fur was completely dry. Bones started to purr.

'Hurry, Atticus!' Callie's anguished cry came across the lagoon.

The light above them was orangey-red. 'It's sunset!' Atticus gasped.

'Come, we will help your other friend, the

233

Inspector of Cheddar.' The mermaid flipped herself out of the casket and into the water. 'Climb on my back.'

The two cats did as they were told.

They whizzed through the water, clinging to the mermaid's hair. In a few seconds they had arrived by the rocks where Inspector Cheddar lay.

'Are they all your friends?' The mermaid asked.

'No! At least . . .' Atticus looked around wildly for Zenia Klob. She had disappeared.

'Klob got away,' Mrs Tucker fumed. 'Ginger Biscuit released her.'

'The others are all my friends,' Atticus explained quickly.

'Hmmm,' the mermaid frowned. 'We will catch this Klob and Biscuit later. First we will save the Inspector of Cheddar.'

The mermaid magicked away the ropes that tied the rescuers' hands behind their backs.

'Lift the Inspector of Cheddar into the lagoon,' the mermaid instructed. 'Don't worry.' She smiled at the children. 'I won't let him drown.'

Mrs Tucker and Mrs Cheddar heaved Inspector Cheddar into the lagoon. He looked very sick. His face was green. His eyeballs were twice their normal size. He had two camel humps on his back.

The mermaid raised her hands to her face and blew into her cupped hands. Then she placed them on Inspector Cheddar's head.

Gradually the Inspector's colour returned. His eyeballs subsided. So did his camel humps. He looked completely normal again.

'I'm cured!' he cried, waking up from Zenia's sleeping potion. He ripped off his shoes and socks and checked his foot. 'Even my verruca's gone.' Thank you, mermaid!'

'It's Atticus you should thank,' the mermaid said. 'As should I. Because of him I'm finally free.'

Mr Tucker looked puzzled. 'I'm pleased about that,' he said, 'don't youze get me wrong, but how did that happen?'

'Because Atticus made a selfless wish,' the mermaid explained simply. 'He didn't ask for anything for himself.'

'Pirate lore didn't say anything about that part of the legend,' Mr Tucker told the mermaid.

'That's because pirates are greedy,' the mermaid replied. 'I'm guessing that bit wasn't passed down.'

'Thank you, Atticus!' Callie threw her arms around his neck. 'You were brilliant!'

'You're the best cat in the world!' Michael joined in the hug.

'Of course he is!' So did Mrs Cheddar, Mr and Mrs Tucker and Bones.

Atticus purred throatily.

'Yes, well done, Atticus,' Inspector Cheddar pulled out his notebook. He chewed the end of his pen. 'Can anyone think of anything that rhymes with cat-tastic police sergeant?' he asked, winking at the children.

Everyone laughed.

'You may have one wish, Atticus,' the mermaid said, 'for releasing me. Can you think of something you really want?'

One wish? Atticus thought hard. He had everything he wanted. Then he had an idea. He whispered it to the mermaid.

'Very well.' She smiled.

25

Atticus finished telling the story to Mimi.

It was nearly sunset, two days after their return from Indonesia to Littleton-on-Sea. The two cats were sitting beside the beach hut.

Atticus was glad to be home. Everything was back to normal. The kids were happy. Mrs Cheddar was feeding him too much. And Inspector Cheddar kept telling him to get off the sofa.

'So what did happen to Klob and Biscuit?' Mimi asked.

'The megalodon ate them,' Atticus said.

'The what?'

'It wasn't a shark exactly that came at the end,' Atticus explained. 'It was a sort of dinosaur-shark called a megalodon. The mermaid was so upset that Klob and Biscuit had killed the other sea creatures she told it to hunt them down and swallow them. It was the one sea creature we didn't know about,' Atticus added. 'You remember me saying that Fishhook Frank and me both had the feeling something was watching us in the lagoon?'

'Yes.'

'Well, I think that was it.' Atticus shuddered. 'I tell you, Mimi, it had a mouth as big as a whale. You should have seen its teeth. Jimmy and his gang. Pam even. They just disappeared! Snap! Just like that. Gone!'

Mimi sighed. 'I know they're criminals,' she said, 'but I'm not sure they deserved to die.'

'Oh, none of them are dead,' Atticus reassured her. 'Not even the magpies. The mermaid told us. The megalodon will just keep them in its stomach for a bit, to give them a fright. It's like being in prison apparently. Now that the mermaid's free, he'll spit them all out when he's had enough of them.'

'But what will they eat?' Mimi asked.

'Oh, you know, mackerel, prawns. That sort of thing. A bit like Pinocchio, when he got stuck in the whale.'

'Oh,' Mimi said. 'Well I suppose that's okay.' She changed the subject. 'When will I meet Bones?'

'Tomorrow,' Atticus promised. 'You'll love her. She's great. She and Mr Tucker have gone out for a sail in the *Destiny* with Callie and Michael and the kittens. They'll have the best time, I know they will. I might even go with them tomorrow.'

'I'm so happy you're back!' Mimi's golden eyes met his.

'So am I!' Atticus twined his tail around hers. 'I love it here.' He gazed across the flat beach. 'It's my home. Now tell me about Aysha's baby.'

'She's adorable!' Mimi laughed. 'Her skin's so soft and she has this wonderful fluffy hair, almost like kitten fur!'

'Er . . . talking of kittens,' Atticus said. 'Well, you know how Pam and Jimmy got married . . .'

'Yes,' Mimi said.

'Well, I wondered if we could, you know, not get married exactly but, well, you know, go out or something?' Atticus stammered. 'And then maybe next time I have an adventure, you could come with me, like you did last time? I'd really like that,' he finished lamely.

Mimi thought for a minute. Then she gave him a kiss with her cold wet nose. 'So would I,' she said.

'Really?' Atticus could hardly believe it. He really was the luckiest cat alive!

'Of course. Now, are you going to show me how to swim or what?' Mimi asked bravely.

'Tomorrow!' Atticus said. 'Right now, I just want to go for a stroll and watch the sunset with you.'

'Beach or town?' Mimi smiled.

'Definitely beach!' Atticus said. 'We might see the mermaid.'

'Oh I'd love that!' Mimi said. 'I wish we could.'

Atticus grinned to himself. He had a wonderful surprise planned for her. He was glad he'd chosen the right wish.

The two cats strolled along the sand, looking out to sea until the sun went down. And just when night came and everything was black and brown like Atticus and the moon shone down on the flat

calm sea, the beautiful mermaid granted his
wish: she swam up to the shore, popped
her head out of the sea and told them
the most wonderful stories that Atticus
and Mimi had ever heard.

FIND OUT WHAT ELSE ATTICUS
HAS BEEN UP TO . . .

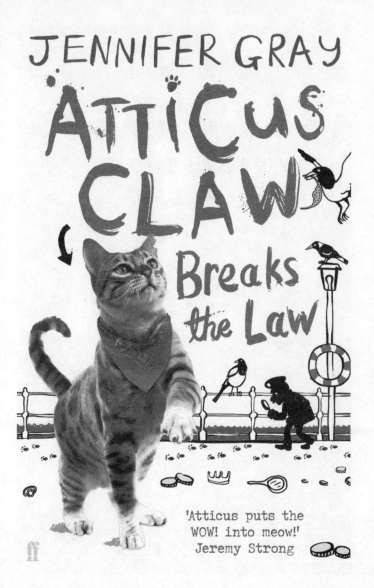

JENNIFER GRAY

ATTICUS CLAW

Breaks the Law

'Atticus puts the
WOW! into meow!'
Jeremy Strong

ff

JENNIFER GRAY

ATTiCUS CLAW

Lends a Paw

'Atticus puts the WOW! into
meow!' Jeremy Strong

AND DON'T MISS . . .
A BRAND NEW SERIES FROM
JENNIFER GRAY, ABOUT
KUNG-FU CHICKENS ON A
TOP-SECRET MISSION!

JENNIFER GRAY

Chicken Mission

Danger in the
Deep Dark Woods

JENNIFER GRAY

WINNER Red House Children's Book Award

Chicken Mission

The Curse of Fogsham Farm